A Brief Setup

Molly quickly locked her phone to hide the mommy-domme video as Ben entered the genetics lab.

"You're not supposed to eat in here, you know." She said curtly.

"Your experiments and everything are like 50 feet away. I think i'll be alright. He mumbled between bites of his sandwich.

Molly sighed and returned to her work, carefully examining sequences on the computer.

She'd been lucky to land this job creating experimental genetically engineered cures and treatments, but had been unlucky with her research associate. Here she was, a doctor, creating experimental cures to real-world diseases; cures that might never see the light of day….and her teammate was a C- student with a bad attitude and horrible work ethic. If thhat wasn't bad enough, she found him 'cute'.

She shuddered as she said the word in her head. How could she find someone so lazy and slovenly cute? *I suppose it's simple*, she thought *He buckles and shrinks at any sign of resistance. He panics if I so much as raise an eyebrow. He's a total submissive, and I'm a total domme. It's only natural. God, what's wrong with me?!*

She turned and looked at Ben. He was at least six inches shorter than her, and as skinny as a twig. She couldn't help but think that she'd easily be able to overpower him. As often happened, an invasive thought of him squirming in a set of bed restraints flitted through her mind. She chased the image away just for another one to replace it. *He's so cute and helpless. I just…want to make him mine. Completely and hopelessly mine.*

Suddenly a thought flew through her mind. It led to another thought, then another. It couldn't be that easy could it? Her mind began to fizz and bubble with plans, scenes, and activities. A cascade of thoughts in a feedback loop kept repeating themselves, each time adding more possibilities and fantasies.

She picked up a syringe and went to the walk-in fridge.

Thousands of bottles and vials lined the walls and filled shelves and drawers. She walked along a shelf, running her finger over the labels, before finally selecting a small vial. It was perfect. The only problem was…could she actually do it? Once she'd done what she had planned there'd be no turning back.

She gulped, screwed up her courage, and filled the syringe with a single CC of the liquid. She paused, thought, and withdrew 3 more CCs. Better safe than sorry.

"Ben, can you bring me the last test results from my office across the hall?" She asked timidly

Ben sighed and put down his sandwich. "Sure." He said, spewing a few crumbs from his mouth as he said the word.

As soon as he left, Molly rushed forward, and squirted the syringe contents into his water bottle. Her stomach was churning and she felt lightheaded with anxiety and excitement. She sat down at the computer and tried to clear her mind, but it was too full of fantasies.

She bit her lip and butterflies filled her stomach as she heard Ben enter, walk back to the counter, and drink several large gulps from his water bottle.

Ch 1: A Horrible Morning

I finished my sandwich and chugged my water. It had a weird chlorinated taste to it that I chalked up to a bad filter in the drinking fountain where i'd filled it.

Molly had her back to me and was hard at work flipping through her papers, and typing away at the computer. "Why's she always so cranky?" I thought as I tossed my wrapper away.

"Hey, it's five, I'm heading out. Need me to do anything before I leave?" I called from across the lab.

"No thankyou. Have a good night!" she answered.

Strange, she was smiling so much. She must have seen some results on the genetic markers she was working with.

Eager to leave work, i grabbed my backpack and hastily made my way to the bus stop. I felt a my stomach gurgle a little but thought nothing of it at the time. I reached the bus stop only a couple minutes before the bus, and soon I was on my way back to my apartment.

Safe within the confines of my own room, I suddenly felt an urge to pee out of nowhere. It was like nothing i'd ever felt before. One minute I was sitting down in my office chair, preparing to do some light gaming, and the next I was rushing to the bathroom as if I'd needed to pee all day long. I undid the button of my jeans as I ran to the bathroom, and only barely made it to the toilet before the dam burst and I began peeing.

"That was weird" was my only thought as i gave my member the usual shake before rezipping my pants and returning to my PC.

I played a my game all evening until late that night. I didn't think anything of my frequent needs to go to the bathroom. It was normal for me to lose track of the time and game until nature called. However, What i didn't notice at the time was that my bathroom breaks were becoming more and more frequent. I had also been drinking lots of energy drinks while I gamed, so frequent urination wasn't something out of the norm.

At about midnight I simply undressed to my underwear, and crawled into bed. "Another day at work tomorrow" I sighed to myself as I pulled the blanket over myself. "At least it'll be friday." I thought as I finally drifted off.

I don't remember what I dreamed about. Something to do with waterfalls..or was it boats? I awoke feeling...**WET**?

I threw the blanket off my body and looked down at the huge wet spot. I was at a loss for words. I hadn't wet the bed since I was a child! Even though I was the only one present, I felt ashamed and embarrassed. I just lay there for a minute, taking in the disaster that had occured.

I winced as I moved and felt the shifting of the cold wet wet fabric all around my groin. Eager to not feel it anymore I left the bed, peeled the saturated underwear from my body, and gathered all my bedding into the laundry bin.As I stood there, pondering my next move, I felt the sudden urge to pee again, but before I could move i was forced to watch in horror as a small stream of urine, only lasting a few seconds, flowed from me, completely out of my control.

My mouth dropped open. I was unaware of how comical I must have looked, gawping in shock at my genitals as I peed directly onto the vinyl flooring. As the short flow subsided, and I stood in a puddle of my own making, dread seeped into my soul. I still had work today!

I looked at the clock. 4:00AM. I had to be at the lab at six!

"Maybe I can take a sick day! Or paid leave! Or…" the thoughts were interrupted with the memory that I'd used all my sick days and paid leave…and even been absent from work a few days on top of that. I had two strikes already. If I called out today i'd have to look for another job. There was nothing for it. I HAD to go to work today. How was I going to go to work when I was obviously sick? I calmed myself down and began to think. If I could just make it through work today somehow, I'd for sure recover from this probable food poisoning, and be right as rain by monday.

I began to formulate a plan. If I hurried I could take the bus to the 24-hour pharmacy, get some 'protection' and be at work just in time to clock in.

I quickly dressed, went to the bathroom to make sure my bladder was empty, tnen headed as to the pharmacy. Despite many fears of pissing myself while on the bus, I finally made it, and found myself in the incontinence aisle.

I stood there, blushing crimson as I looked at the many many products. I couldn't believe I was doing this. With massive amounts of mortification I began weighing pros and cons. Did I want something extremely thin that nobody would notice? Or something thick and safe so if I had an accident it wouldn't leak at all?

I decided to split the difference and grab a small pack of pull-on briefs. They just felt the least embarrassing.

My heart was beating so fast as I approached the checkout area. I had hoped to use the self checkout machines, but my heart nearly stopped when I saw that they were all closed. I had no choice but to shamefully purchase the briefs from a cashier.

Our interaction was beyond awkward. I felt her size me up, and noticed the glance down then up as she surveyed the incontinent young man in front of her,

"M-my grandpa ran out of …these" I mumbled.

"Mhmm" she said, clearly not buying my story."Receipt?"

"N-no thanks, I-" My eyes shot open and I screamed internally as for a brief moment I felt a sudden intense urge to pee, followed by a spreading warmth. I saw her glance downward as I grabbed the bag and held it in front of the damp spot in my pants.

"You *snicker* should probably get those to your "grandpa" soon!" She covered her mouth with a hand, but it was clear she was desperately trying to suppress a loud and long laugh.

I ran to the store bathroom and raced into a stall, ripping open the package of briefs and yanking out a pair.

I was so desperate I didn't even hesitate as I pulled the crinkling object up over my damp skin and over my flaccid member. I took some deep breaths and tried to think about my next steps.

The pants are kinda dark and the spot isn't TOO big. As long as I cover my crotch with papers or my backpack, and I sit down under a desk most of the day I can still pull this off!

I opened my backpack, it was full of papers, binders, my laptop and other things I needed. There was no room to store any extra briefs. While I hated to waste them, I left them in the stall and quickly left the store.

With any luck this would be my last time wearing one of these!

It felt strange under my clothing as I boarded the bus, Every movement caused a faint crinkling. I was almost sure everyone around me knew I was wearing what was basically an adult pullup. I peeked under my backpack at the wet spot.

Dry faster!

I'd hoped that over the course of the day that the food poisoning would stop, but the painful need to pee, followed shortly by release seemed to be happening more frequently. I was starting to worry about the capacity of my protection. When I moved I could feel it swinging between my legs slightly, and it had stopped crinkling. I didn't dare squeeze my legs together. Just from walking I knew how squishy and full the pullup had become. I was in a constant state of worry that Molly would notice or smell the urine.

I'd almost made it through the end of the day when we were cleaning out some beakers.

 "Ben, can you bring me more soap from the closet? This one is empty."

"Of course!"

I walked as normally as I could, and was on my way back with the soap when my heart stopped, and I froze. Something new…something BAD was happening. I opened my mouth in absolute shock and horror as I felt a sudden urge to poop, followed immediately by my body's betrayal.

I couldn't even remember what this had felt like as a child. I just froze as the seemingly never ending log pushed out, pushing out the back of my pullup before crumpling into a soft mass. I also felt small streams of wet running down my legs. A loud wet fart erupted from me as another, looser mass joined the first, filling up every nook and cranny of my already thoroughly used pullup.

Fuck fuck fuck fuck!

"Ben? Are you-oh my god!" Molly exclaimed as she watched me, knees slightly bent as i pissed and shit myself right in front of her.

"Molly, I-I"

"The bathrooms are RIGHT next door!" she exclaimed in disbelief.

"I'm sorry! I just-I can't help it!" tears started to form and my voice cracked as the stream of feces finally ended in a loud wet fart, now muffled by my full pullup.

In tears, I explained everything that had been happening, and that I'd probably eaten something bad, and it was just food poisoning. When I finished she put her finger on her chin in a pose indicative of deep thought.

"Y'know…food poisoning wouldn't cause a problem with urination…we've been working on all kinds of dangerous 'gene-editors'…mostly used for de-aging specific parts of the face via subcutaneous injection for cosmetic purposes."

"Yeah, so?"

"Suppose someone kept eating in the lab, and *INGESTED* it, exposing all kinds of non-facial organs to it. All the cells in your digestive tract and various systems could have ben permanently altered"

"Permanently?!" I once again felt a slow, creeping feeling of dread crawl into my soul.

"Well, without research to undo it…which would cost upwards of several million dollars," She straightened up. Lay down on the table, We need to check something.

I was in shock and reeling at even the suggestion that i was now permanently incontinent through my own carelessness. I felt numb as she led me to the stainless steel counter and helped me onto it. I felt her undo the button on my pants.

"No, you can't-"

She swatted my hands away easily and yanked my pants down, exposing my saturated pullup, now expanded far beyond what it was designed to manage.

"I'm a doctor, probably the only doctor in the world that has even a marginal chance of understanding what's been done. To do that I need to perform a physical."

"Can't I clean up first?" I begged, well aware of how whiny I sounded.

"I need to also see the color, smell, and consistency of your waste. If any of your organs are damaged or not functioning, that could be a clue. Still, I need your permission. May i inspect…***this***" She motioned to the general area of my pullup.

"I-I guess" I mumbled feebly. I wanted to be invisible. A beautiful woman, a woman I respected and found extremely attractive was now going to see my piss and shit covered body.

"Then let's get on with your diaper change." She said it as a statement of fact. It wasn't until 30 seconds or so later that I realized that she'd referred to my protection as a diaper. By then she'd already cut the sides of the pullup and pulled the front down, exposing my shriveled penis to the cold air of the lab.

"Pee yoo! What did you eat!" she said loudly. She said it in such a cute silly voice. I wanted to die.

"Well, no dark, bloody, or off-colored things. Looks relatively healthy down here. She grabbed a paper towel and began to clean me as best as she could with no baby-wipes around. I felt so infantile. It didn't help that she crossed my ankles and lifted my butt up so she could wipe me better. She did it so easily and curtly, like it was nothing to her!

Once I was mostly clean, she wet a paper towel, added a little hand soap and began to clean me more thoroughly. The warm soapy towel felt…good. TOO GOOD!

I panicked as i felt a familiar little throb, and my penis began to grow.

Please God no! Please no! Don't do it!

She pretended not to notice until I was sporting a full erection.

"What have we here! Is baby's little friend saying hello?"

I said nothing, I just turned yet another deeper shade of red as humiliation burned within me.

"Does he want to shake hands?" She wrapped the soapy paper towel around my member and began to stroke it quickly. This action surprised me and I let out a moan at the sudden burst of pleasure.

"Looks like the baby's getting all excited!"

I was getting close. I couldn't believe what was happening. I strained against the building pressure. I couldn't do this! It was too much! Despite all my internal conflict, i was moaning and twitching.

I felt some fingers pushing my mouth open. I obeyed automatically and opened my mouth for her fingers, just to have a metal piece of lab equipment jammed into my mouth, holding it open.

My hips thrust a final time as my orgasm swept through me. In a single fluid motion similar to how she'd lifted my legs to clean me, she now had my legs up over my head.

I looked with surprise and disgust at my own penis, now mere inches from my face as I came.

"Uuuk! Uuuuuguuk!" I shouted as I watched my penis cum directly into my mouth and across my face. Rope after rope hit the metal makeshift gag, and dribbled into my mouth. The salty, musky taste filled my nostrils and mouth. I wanted to swallow, but couldn't with my mouth held open. The cum just collected at the back of my throat.

Molly lowered my legs. When I tried to remove the test-tube holder in my mouth she batted my hands away.

"Your physical isn't over." She simply said. As she lubed her fingers with some of the cum on my face. "You can wash your face off later."

"Uuh!" I grabbed the table edges and tried to sit up as I felt fingers press against my anus.

"Sit still."

"AAUGH!" I gurgled with a mouth full of cum and saliva. Her finger was now inside of me.

"I want you to squeeze your little hole like you're stopping yourself from making poopies. Can you do that, baby?" She said condescendingly.

Utterly beaten and humiliated I did as she asked and clenched.

"Auugmm!" I felt two more fingers stretching my virgin hole open.

"Again."

Again I clenched down as hard as I could. And again I felt her shift and add another finger, then push firmly.

"AUUGGHGH" I gurgled as I felt four fingers ream into me, stretching me open further than I'd ever felt before. Again she asked me to clench, and again I'd done it.

I went limp as I felt the relief of her retreating fingers. Soon i was empty in every sense, limply lying naked from the waist down on the cold steel of the lab. I was thankful that the two of us were the only ones ever in here.

Molly talked as she left me to retrieve something from the storage cabinets.

"Even with four fingers into you, buried as far as I dared, I felt nothing when you clenched. Nothing whatever. Your stool was mostly solid, so it's not diarrhea from food poisoning."

She returned with a large garbage bag that she began rummaging through. I supposed that we were just going to pretend that she hadn't made me cum into my mouth, and then rammed half her hand into me.

"Whatever you were exposed to obviously hasn't affected any major organs in any critical way. But what it HAS affected, it's done so by changing your genes. I'm sorry but it's most likely permanent. I guess you've learned the hard way why you're not supposed to eat inside the-Ah! here they are!"

My eyes nearly popped out of my head when she withdrew a package…of diapers! Pink diapers! She noticed and explained as she pulled the makeshift gag from my mouth, allowing me to finally swallow the foul salty mixture that had been collecting in the back of my throat.

"Several years ago we had a study that focused on chimps. This bag is what remains from that experiment. The scientist used blue and pink diapers to tell what sex was which, while also preventing accidents all over the lab."

"And the blue ones?"

"As luck would have it, there aren't any of those in here."

"Of course not." I said sourly.

She lifted my legs and slid the unfolded diaper under me. I winced as I was lowered onto it. It crinkled like 5 tons of tissue paper, and was thicker than five pairs of pants all at once. I felt a small prick on my scrotum but thought nothing of it. I didn't see her subtly remove and hide the syringe.

She pulled the front of the diaper up between my legs. It was so thick and compact that it felt stiff, and pushed my legs out to the sides.

She took my hand and pulled me up to a sitting position. Now that I was clean and not naked I felt some of my old self and some bravery return.

"So, based on nothing but that single test you think i'm permanently incontinent? You'll excuse me if I don't believe you." I couldn't and wouldn't believe her diagnosis.

"Suit yourself, but maybe you should bring a bunch of these diapers with you just in case…for over the weekend."

"I'm pretty sure I won't need them after today. At least I hope not. Besides, my backpack is full, and there's no way I'm walking out of here with an arm full of pink diapers." I stated firmly.

She smiled, picked up my backpack, opened it, removed a stack of binders, replaced them four diapers, zipped the backpack up, and then handed me the binders. I am such an idiot.

She laughed for the first time since I'd met her, and said "How have you survived this long?"

"You're enjoying this." i said glumly.

"To be honest, yes I am. Also, if you don't mind me saying so, you look adorable in diapers!"

"Stop it!"

"I could just eat you up!" She laughed, teasing me in a baby voice dripping with condescension

"Stop it! I-Is that the time?! I'm going to miss my bus! What will i wear! I can't go on the bus with just a shirt and a diaper!!"

"Calm down! I have a spare outfit I keep here that you can wear, you may not like it, but it's better than your current outfit!"

She walked to a closet, removed a garment bag and unzipped it. My mouth dropped open, You'd think by then I would've gotten used to shocking and horrible surprises. But at the realization i'd have to wear what she was holding I felt queasy and bit my lip.

"We'll, step in!" She said, holding it out for me to enter.

"I-I- but, but-" I stammered desperately.

"Get over here, or I'll take this dress back and you can go ride the bus in just your diaper."

"No! I-i'll do it."

I approached the pink object like it was a dangerous animal. I looked down into the pink maw stretched open before me and lowered a leg through the garment. I felt like I was having an out-of-body experience as Molly pulled the elastic waist up my legs, and felt the soft loose material brush against my legs.

I looked down to see a skirt ending at my mid-thigh. As long as nobody was shorter than me, and there was no wind, my diaper would remain a secret.

"Now the front!" Molly said excitedly. I hadn't noticed there was a front!

Folded down in front of the skirt was an overall-like dress front that she raised up over my white T-shirt. Some overall straps were pulled over my shoulders. I was frozen in a cocktail of emotions, fears, and horrors as the straps were connected to the dress front. When she was finished, she straightened the skirt then stepped back to look at me critically.

"Hmm…you're missing…*something.*"

She removed her white hairband and placed it on my head, before toying with my hair, moving and arranging individual strands. I was too flustered to say anything, I just stood there, feeling like a girl's Barbie doll.

"God! YOU'RE SO CUTE!" Molly was practically jumping up and down.

Despite the massive amounts of humiliation, being told I was cute by a beautiful woman made my heart flutter a little.

"Really?" I said softly, still in shock from recent events.

"Yes! You look like the cutest little baby girl in the world!"

"I'm a boy!" I protested, realizing how infantile I sounded as the words left my lips. "And I don't need this headband!"

"I said you looked LIKE a baby girl" She said. "And the headband completes the look."

There were an awkward few moments where she eyed me up and down, biting her lip. Did she like this? All indicators showed that she found my current state highly arousing.

"My bus!" I gathered my belongings as quickly as I could and ran out the door.

I sprinted out of the building and to the bus stop. I probably looked sunburned. I was so red. My cheeks felt like they were on fire as I climbed onto the bus.

As I looked down, I saw that the diaper, which had been tightly compacted into a flat layer in the package, had been "fluffed" by my run, and was now nearly twice as puffy. The bottom of the diaper was clearly visible.

Fuck why me? Why? God, just let my humiliation end!

The seats were full. I had to stand. I pulled my dress down in the front, and felt the back lift.

I pulled down on the back and front, but it was no use. I felt the gaze of dozens of strangers eying me, and heard a few giggles.

Hssss My eyes bulged as I felt the diaper warm and expand. I hadn't even felt the need to go! I broke into a cold sweat. There was no way others around me weren't hearing me audibly soaking my embarrassingly large diaper.

I finally made it home, completely and utterly drained, physically and emotionally. I heated up some dinner and sat in front of my gaming PC.

In the reflection of the powered-down screen I saw a pretty girl. The dress was so infantile. I guess my face really was androgynous enough to appear male or female depending on the context. Molly was right I looked…*shudder* cute.

But what was all that stuff on- MY FACE! I had forgotten to wash my face before I left work!

I groaned. What a day. What a weird day. Hopefully Molly was wrong about this being permanent. She had to be wrong. I HAD to regain control somehow.

I got a text alert from my phone and looked at it.

Hey. Hope ur okay. I know this was a rough day for you. Hopefully the kinky bit helped.

You know the funny thing? It did help a little. I'd never been very kinky, but It was the best part of my day…even if the taste had been horrible. The text was quickly followed by another one.

Pls let me know if I crossed a line. I thought you could use some fun and cheering up. From gured I might as well. A handjob from a coworker ranks way lower than a diaper change imo. You can keep the dress btw. It looks better on you.

She'd definitely crossed a few dozen professional lines, but somehow I had…liked it? Even though I hadn't? Losing control over the situation and letting Molly completely take over had felt weird…but good?

I had never had any kinks that I knew about before, but to have all that happen so quickly…I felt like a pre-fire caveman who'd just been shown a flamethrower, or like one of the Wright brothers flying in a fighter jet.

I sighed and collapsed onto the bed.

Ch 2 A Sissy by Design

Watching my baby waddle-run to the bus with a face-full of cum was probably the cutest thing i'd ever seen. In fact, the whole day had been incredible, I was absolutely in love with my new engineered role as a sissy mommy.

I knew he was submissive…but WOW! He'd let me go so much further than I thought he would. This boy was going to make a bigger sissy than any fictional sissy i'd ever seen in porn. How had I not done this earlier! Here i was reading and watching erotica and porn involving pseudosciences like hypnosis and magic feminization potions, when i'd had the means and ability to create a sissy completely from scratch!

The explanation I had given him for his incontinence had been a lie, of course. the belief that his digestive system had regressed due to a feminine cosmetic gene therapy would pave the way for his inevitable feminization. The truth was less charming. I'd given him a therapy reserved for causing complete incontinence in lab rats for digestive surveys. It was completely permanent. My poor baby would be filling his pampers for the rest of his life,

I cleaned the lab and then drove home. A short dinner later, and a nice long session with my vibrator, I found myself reading through the dose of modifications i'd injected him with during his diaper change,

837516=782A: Potential cure for anorgasmia pending further trials and reviews. All tests indicate treatment will result in decreased time to climax, increased sensitivity, increased libido, and highly improved ejaculate volume & sperm production

I closed my eyes…I could just see my little sissy, rock hard in his diaper, flooding his padding with his own juices, just from the stimulation of the diaper on his little clitty. I couldn't wait to run my hands over his crinkly diaper, just to tease him for instantly spurting his load in a pathetically joyless premature ejaculation. I'd have this boy begging for the safety of a chastity cage just to stop his poor little clitty from uncontrollably pumping his cream into his thirsty diapers.

97580-7G: Potential cure for dysgeusia. May be modified following procedure 867431-201 to enhance, eliminate, or substitute specific perceptions of taste.

Ah, this one had been more complicated. I'd been up all thursday night in the lab, working with expired semen samples from the fertility wing. If i had it right, most of his taste receptors would be programmed to taste ONLY the elements of semen. My sissy was going to learn to crave his own milkies and others' cummies as the only source of flavor. Of course, I could reverse it once he'd fully accepted a diet of cum flavors.

My head was swimming with possibilities for how to introduce Ben to his first real cock. Maybe I could just do them all?

0956120-12-523-7A: Potential body dysmorphia hormone replacement therapy alternative (MTF). Targeted cells responsible for the majority of feminization goals in trans women will be edited to switch functions for estrogen and testosterone receptors. Potential effects include breast tissue growth, lip growth, facial restructuring, and body fat redistribution.

I giggled as I read the synopsis. I could just picture him now as a total femboy sporting cute little boobies and a feminine frame. I couldn't wait. Unlike the first two, I'd have to wait a while for this one to take effect. The other two could happen rapidly. Overnight even. The best part, an endocrinologist, if Ben saw one, would prescribe testosterone, only increasing the effect!

8566352-078Bi: potential treatment for babies unable to 'latch' for breastfeeding. Reversible when 8566352-078BJ is applied. Use outside of infants highly likely to cause intense oral fixations.

I could just see him now, never content or satisfied without something to suck on…gratefully suckling a pacifier, bottle, boob, or dick, and completely baffled as to why he felt anxious without something to slobber on.

I was too excited. Maybe another session with mvibrator...By now Ben would be home, and probably in need of some kind words of comfort. I picked up my phone and sent him a couple kind messages. He'd need a lot of kind support this first weekend as he finally came to terms with his incontinence.

Ch 3: A Long Weekend

I awoke to a completely saturated diaper, which would have immediately crushed my hopes that my wetting problem was due to food poisoning…but something else was taking precedence. My mind was on fire, burning with white-hot arousal that had seemingly come from nowhere.

I threw off the blanket, revealing the pink dress i'd gone to bed in. I'd been far too tired to change clothes. I pulled the skirt up and could see my erection throbbing under the thick soggy pink diaper. How could I be turned on by this?! It had to be normal morning wood, right?

I moved my hips slightly and couldn't help but immediately moan as a warm, wet diaper made incredibly slick with precum rubbed against the head of my eager penis. The feeling was incredible, far more intense than it had any right to be. I'd been masturbating for years, but no amount of lotion and hand-action could compare with how this currently felt.

I slowly pushed my hips up into the air. My cock shifted, and the head slipped against the heavy, precum lubricated interior of the diaper.

"Ooh!" I exclaimed with surprise. Only a single thrust and i'd felt a small little spurt of precum, joining the pool in the diaper.

I lowered my hips back into the mattress. My penis slipped back to its resting position in the diaper and I gasped as the intense pleasure nearly overwhelmed me.

I couldn't help myself. I knew i'd hate myself for it afterward, but an animalistic urge took over. I rolled over onto my stomach, placed my hands under my crotch, and began to hump with my hands through the diaper. The sensations were other-worldly. I wanted it to continue forever, but within what was probably only a matter of seconds, I felt myself suddenly climaxing. I had never cum like this before in my life. As spasms of pleasure took control of me, I could **hear** the spurts and the jets of my cum in the diaper. This wasn't just the usual teaspoon or two of jizz…I could **feel** it soaking my crotch, and running down my balls to eventually be absorbed by the diaper.

hss-hss-hss-hss

Every spurt was accompanied by a completely uncontrolled shaky thrust against my diaper and a spasm of ecstasy. I thought I was going to pass out! Eventually I came down from my high, and lifted my head from the pillow that i'd been moaning into. The pillowcase was wet with drool.

I rolled back onto my stomach, my slippery heavy diaper making a 'shlick'. I reached for my phone to browse the web, I had to take my mind off of my current situation. I was surprised to see that i'd already received a few more early-morning texts from Molly.

Good morning, cutie!

I didn't want to say anything yesterday, but i totally had you pegged as a sissy baby months ago. I bet you've already cum in your diapers, and it was far better than any orgasm you've ever had!

My mouth dropped open. How did she know?! I wasn't a sissy! Or a baby!

In fact, I wouldn't be surprised if you're still wearing the little pink dress!

I looked down at the dress. Fuck.

If you need help accepting your new life please don't hesitate to text me for advice/support. It would be my honor to be your mommy. It can be a lonely life for a cute little baby like you

I had no idea what to say to any of that. Do I risk insulting one of the only women NOT put off by a man in diapers by insisting she's wrong? Best to remain polite but indifferent. I responded:

Thanks! I'll let you know. Your support and help means a whole lot to me.

Within seconds she sent me another text:

Lol, I notice you didn't deny making cummies in your diaper or wearing your pretty dress. Just make sure to shave everything next time you change. It'll make our daily diaper change sessions easier. Babies shouldn't have to change themselves!

I packed you two diapers. Try to make them last until monday!

Gotta go! Try not to just fill your diaper with sissy cream all weekend!

What the fuck. Daily changes?! Where did she get off assuming that i'd be down for that! And that i'd shave my pubes on her whim?

That final text made me reflect on that wonderful orgasm. My cock twitched and i felt a little growth from it. No! I wasn't going to hump my diaper again! I was going to make breakfast like a normal person!

I stood up and moaned, and my legs shook a little as I waddled in my soaked diaper. Every movement caused a level of pleasure that made my mind go blank momentarily.

I would need to change first. This diaper was too…slimy, disgusting, and…stimulating.

The diaper hit the bathroom tiles with a squishy thud.

After a quick shower I was in a fresh, dry diaper and some sweatpants that did nothing to hide the infantile bulk. This was better! Dry, crinkly, and flaccid!

As soon as I thought the words, a small stream of hot urine trickled around my crotch and I felt my cock pulse. How was I this turned on by wet diapers?

It was strange. Although I didn't fully notice it at the time, if I didn't focus, I found my mouth moving in an agitated way. I kept sucking on my tongue, pursing and biting my lips like there was something missing from my mouth.

While eating my cereal I kept 'losing' the spoon only to find that it was still in my mouth where I was sucking on it. It felt calming to me and right somehow. Additionally, breakfast tasted bland, like all the flavors had been diluted or something.

I tried to go back to my normal routine. I booted up my PC to play some games, I found that after every match or level I'd be frantically rubbing by diaper front into a life-shattering orgasm, and I had been sucking on a pen for hours. It wasn't until the afternoon and several orgasms later that I felt another urge. I barely had time to stand and run a few steps toward the bathroom before I felt the hot mush push my diaper out.

Something was wrong though. This movement was more solid than yesterday's and the pressure from the diaper was preventing me from finishing the bowel movement. What was I supposed to do when I was being held open by waste I couldn't expell? I stood there and strained as hard as I could. Nothing.

How did babies do it? I cringed as I lowered myself to a low squat and stuck my butt out. I strained. I was 'rewarded' with a surge of thick feces that exploded out of me with a sickening wet fart. Despite my disgust, my penis pulsed out a droplet of precum and I, captive to my whims, sank to the floor where I humped my slimy laden diaper until completion.

I just laid there on the floor in perverse fascination at what I'd become, sucking fervently on the pen as tears rolled silently down my cheeks. What had I become?!

To make matters worse, I now had a choice, remain in this diaper until tomorrow to evenly ration my diapers until Monday? Or should I change now and try to make it 36 whole hours in the last diaper?

As I stood I felt the cum run down my crotch to gather at the bottom of the diaper, and felt the mass shift, rubbing against my balls. Staying in this mess overnight was NOT an option. I waddled into the bathroom and began the long process of cleaning myself. I gagged several times from the smell.

I thought of her text "babies shouldn't have to change themselves!" I hated this. It HAD been easier to just lie there and let her clean me. She hadn't even looked grossed out..more *proud* of me, which was odd. I found myself wishing she were here to just do it for me, and forced myself not to think anymore about that.

"I'm *NOT* her baby! I'm an adult, I can take care of myself!" I shouted internally.

I taped myself into the final dry diaper, happy to finally feel dry again. I just had to make it until Monday. I could do that, right? Worst-case scenario, I'd return to the pharmacy tomorrow and purchase some more.

To rid my apartment of the smell I took out the garbage containing my diapers. I felt better now that I wasn't smelling pee and feces.

For lunch/dinner I ordered a pizza, which tasted almost as bland as breakfast. It was like they only added a quarter of the seasonings or something. At least it was food. I returned to my game and found myself taking breaks just to put something in my mouth. I was full, but it just felt nice to take big bites of food and play with them. Running my tongue over the food and sucking on it. Has eating like this always felt comforting?

Before I knew it, my hand returned to the box to find emptiness. I'd finished the entire pizza, and my stomach felt distended and full. With cold realization I knew that what went in had to come out eventually.

My phone dinged. Another message from Molly.

Just bought some gifts for you! Excited to see you Monday! How're the diapers holding up?

I responded curtly:

Good. Cleanup sucks though.

She responded 15 minutes later:

Sorry baby! Mommy will take care of you first thing Monday morning!

I didn't respond. I wished I were as into this as she was. I tossed my phone onto the bed and returned to my game as my diaper dampened.

I wish I could say that I made it all day and night without humping a wet diaper, but once it was damp and slick I found myself humping tables, chairs, pillows, my hands, even the floor. Sometimes I'd stop playing just to rub my diaper-front to orgasm, much to my team's anger.

At midnight, as I was about to power down my PC, I felt my anus open to deposit the pizza I'd had for lunch.

No! I couldn't sleep in this! I sat firmly on the chair. If I maintained pressure on my butt, maybe I could hold it in.

I sat on my hands, desperately trying to hold the escaping mess inside myself as a stream of urine released in concert with my inevitable bowel movement. I could feel the pressure building as I frantically fought for some level of control.

A sneeze caught me off guard. Instantly all hell broke loose. With all the pressure on the back of my diaper there was only one place for the disgusting waste to go.

I screamed and broke into tears as the surge of thick warm feces flooded the front of my final diaper.

My cock, upon feeling the soft wet warmth squish around it, went to full mast and began pulsing expectantly.

I slowly made my way to the bed. If I just slept Monday would come sooner. I dred my eyes, sniffling only a bit, and laid down on my back slowly and carefully. I ignored the intense horniness and sensations from my insistent genitals and eventually somehow managed to sleep.

I dreamed that there was a beautiful woman, naked and on all fours, begging me to cum in her. When I looked down I found that my penis was hard, dripping, and massive. The rest of the dream was hours upon hours of thrusting into her ass and pussy, and having orgasm after orgasm.

I awoke face-down on the mattress to the comforting feeling of sucking on something. As I opened my eyes I found my thumb deep within my mouth, pink and wrinkled like a raisin from what must have been hours of sucking on it

My cock felt so incredibly good, it was straining hard in the warm slimy mush. in my barely-conscious seepy haze I thought of that sexy ass and began to thrust, barely remembering, and not caring about what I was *actually* having sex with.

In my post-nut clarity everything came back to me and I began to cry with my thumb still in my mouth. Even though it made me feel more ridiculously infant-like, the thought of removing my thumb caused me to feel anxious.

The beginning of the day was similar to yesterday. I made an omelet with peppers, cheese, and tomatoes. Unfortunately, when I took a bite it tasted as bland as the pizza yesterday. I added more hot sauce..still bland. I added more…it was only slightly spicy. I took a direct hit of the hot sauce. It was the taste equivalent of hearing music through a long tunnel. I could just barely taste the heat and flavor I should have. I added the rest of the bottle and finished my disappointing meal.

I needed out of this diaper. I waddled to the bathroom, my sagging padding slapping against my thighs.i ripped off the tapes and winced as it hit the ground with a splat. After a quick shower I sat on the toilet.

"No need for protection as long as I stay here." I thought as I heard the tinkle of urine.

I browsed social media on my phone and watched videos for hours. My legs fell asleep. Pins and needles set in, and my toes felt numb, eventually I ran out of positions for my legs. My porcelain chair became torture. I needed to leave it, but my only other option was my highly used pink diaper.

I tentatively left the toilet, barely able to stand on my numb legs.

I almost gagged as I began doing my best to clean the diaper by scooping my waste from the diaper to the toilet. Eventually i had most of my waste down the toilet

I then quickly retrieved some duct tape from the hall closet to replace the ripped tapes.

I laid the smelly object on the floor, and my stomach churned and I gazed at the disgusting object I'd be taping myself into.

I stepped over it, crouched, and lined myself up with the wet mess on the floor between my legs. I did my best not to focus on the pungent scent of the filth below as I lowered myself into the diapers interior.

I winced as I sank into the cold wet wet folds. the diaper reacted with a disgusting **SQUELCH** and that was it. The end of my brief reprieve from diapers.

I bit my lip and tried to think of literally anything else as I gently pulled the heavy diaper-front up. My legs splayed out to accept the chilly bulk as it squished against my crotch.

Soon I was standing in front of the bathroom mirror looking at a miserable sissy with a massive over-used pink diaper tightly duct taped around his waist. The foul thing kept slipping down and slopping against my thighs.

I pulled it up tightly, and went around and around the waist with yards of duct tape. Cutting it off would be the only way to remove it now, since I needed protection for the bus ride tomorrow, I was now trapped in this soggy crotch-prison until tomorrow morning.

I wet a few more times before bedtime. Through some miracle though, my diaper held the mess

After only an hour or two of sleep I awoke to a stomach gurgling and churning. Cramps wracked my body as I rolled out of bed and sleepily took up the crouching position.

Pthpthpth

Wet hot diarrhea spewed into the diaper at a high velocity, filling it up, both front and back. It was 2am, and I was too tired to care. I returned to my bed, stuck my thumb in my mouth, and softly humped my own wet waste until my orgasm finally put me to sleep.

Ch 4: Monday Funday

I almost gasped when I saw Ben Monday morning. He slunk into the lab amid the stench of a well-used diaper. His eyes were red, and his the bulk of his diaper pressed tightly against his sweatpants. You could tell he was a diaper from half a mile away.

His cheeks burned red as he waddled up to me. He sniffed as he asked in a whisper; "m-may I please have a fresh diaper?"

"Of course, sweetie!"

I patted the metal counter, and he slowly climbed onto it, into the position of his last change.

I pulled off his pants, noticing all the wet spots where he'd leaked through the legs of his diaper.

"Pee too! Baby certainly used his diaper thoroughly!" I beamed as he covered his face in his hands. Embarrassing him was just too fun.

"Did somebody learn that it's best when Mommy does the changes?" I asked in a pitying tone.

Abashed silence was my only answer.

"If the baby wants a crinkly new dipee he'd better respond!"

"Y-yes."

"Yes, who?"

"Yes…Mommy."

I began wiping him down. I'd have to punish him for not shaving, but that'd come later. I had more questions for my sissy.

"Tell me, did you wisely ration out your diapers like a responsible adult? Or did you just change yourself twice on Saturday like a foolish little child?"

Silence

"Well?" I asked, pausing my cleanup.

"Th-the latter."

I continued "Did you eat only simple healthy foods to make cleanup easier like a smart capable adult? Or a lot of junk food and spicy cheesy things?"

I could tell from the spicy smell of the diaper and his intense rash that the latter was true.

"Oh my!" I held his hardening cockhead between my thumb and index finger and pulled it out to show the sissy. "Your clitty is so chafed! How many times did you make cummies?!"

Silence.

"I'll take you right back into your diaper if you don't say!" I picked up the diaper front and slowly pulled it toward his crotch.

"No! Wait, Mommy! It-it was a lot!"

"How many?"

"Ili don't know! I lost track!"

"More than a dozen?"

"Yes! Much more! Just please, don't put me back in my mess!

"Wow! Baby just can't control his love for big wet diapers!"

"I do NOT love them! I hate wearing diapers!"

"You do?"

"Yes!"

I said nothing, I just pulled a condom from my purse and slowly rolled it over his shaft.

"Time for a test. I'm going to ask you a few questions. If you can keep from cumming then I'll believe you. If you cum then the only words I want to hear are: 'I'm just a sorry little sissy baby that needs you to be my mommy.' Understood?"

He slowly nodded, uncertain about this new game.

I picked up his used diaper and rolled it into a tube, then shoved it onto his erection. I began to slowly move it up and down like a filthy fleshlight. He squealed and squirmed, aware how unlikely it would be for him to last long enough.

"Tell me. Who wears diapers, sucks their thumb, and isn't responsible enough to feed themselves or properly plan changes?"

He knew exactly the answer. "A baby! A b-ooh-by!" He moaned.

And what do you think loves diapers SO much that they spend a whole weekend humping and cumming in used pink diapers?"

"A sissy! -A sis-mmmoooh!" He was getting close, so I slowed my movement on his cock.

" Who is struggling even now to keep from cumming in a soppy diaper, with his last shred of dignity on the line?

"Me!" He cried as tears filled his eyes.

"And now the final question…" I increased the pressure and speed of my strokes. His hips bucked, his breathing went ragged, and his arms fought for anything to grip.He was losing all capacity for thought

"What are you?"

"I'm- uuaah! I'm a- oouuh! I'm not a-oh God!"

He thrust so hard I to the diaper that the only parts touching the table were his head and heels. He screamed gutterally and sobbed as he pumped a massive, thick load into the condom. God, I was so wet right now.

"Well what are you?"

"Please don't make me!"

"WHAT. ARE. YOU." With each word I drove the diaper Fleshlight down hard, overstimming him so much he screamed

"'I'm just a *sniff* sorry little sissy baby *sob* that needs you to be my mommy!" He wailed.

I removed the diaper, slipped off the condom, and tied a knot in it just above the milky white contents. After I'd cleaned the shit off it I pinched his cheeks to open his mouth, and dropped it into his awaiting mouth. His lips closed around it, the extra length dangling down his chin.

"Suck on your cummy paci like a good boy."

I returned to my task of cleaning him. After I'd finished, I held up his first gift. His eyes went wide and he sucked fervently on the condom. He knew what it was

"Can you keep from making cummies on your own? Or will you make humpies whenever you can?"

"Aw'd make cummieth." He turned bright red at this admission. The condom full of cum filled his mouth, causing the most adorable lisp

"Who are you addressing? I have a name, you know!"

"Aw'd make cummieth…Mommy"

"Good boy. Now. Do you actually WANT to fill your diapers with cum until your little clitty worn down to nothing?"

He shook his head vigorously.

"Then ask nicely for this clitty cage."

He gulped and hesitated briefly. Tears ran down his cheeks as he begged. "Pweathe Mommy. May I pweathe be wicked into thah cwitty cage?"

"Hmm…" I pretended to think about it. Creating the queue for him to expound on that thought

"I-I'm ah wittle babee, an I need a cwitty cage so bad!" He wailed as tears ran down his cheeks.

"How can I refuse my little cutie?" I beamed. I slipped the ring and pink plastic cage over his manhood. With a click his chances of ever cumming like a man ended.

"Before the next gift and a fresh diaper, it's time for your punishment. What did Mommy ask you to do?"

"To shave" he croaked with fear

I helped him up, and gathered a wooden paddle with the word 'BABY' cut out of it from my bag and led him to a stool, where I pulled him over my lap.

"You're about to learn why damp skin makes for a good paddling. After each spank I want you to sincerely thank your mommy for teaching you how to be a good sissy, and count out loud."

I could feel him trembling in fear. I brought the paddle down hard on his left cheek.

CRACK!

The sound was ear-splitting. Ben jumped and screamed bloody-murder, the condom fell from his mouth. The word 'BABY' showed clearly on his cheek.

"Hmm. No count? No thank you? Guess we'll start over."

"No! I-

CRACK!

"AAAAAH! ONE! THANK YOU MOMMY! I'LL SHAVE! I'LL SHAVE EVERYTHING!

CRACK!

"AAAAAUUH! TWO! I'M SO SORRY MOMMY! I'LL NEVER HAVE HAIR THERE AGAIN! I SWEAR! PLEASE JUST-"

CRACK!

AAAAH! *sob* I'LL DO WHATEVER YOU ASK! ALWAYS! PLEEEAAASE!

"Seems like my silly little ditz has already forgotten to-"

"THREE! *sob* THREEEE! THREE MOMMY!"

"Aww, I'm sorry baby, you also forgot to thank me for that spank. We'll just have to start over!"

CRACK!

It ended up taking about twenty spanks for him to finally count to ten. After I'd shaved him completely myself, applied lotion to his rash, and a fresh diaper had been taped onto my sniffling, sobbing sissy, I produced his second gift: a pair of waterproof baby-pink satin diaper covers. They were so puffy and frilled that at first he didn't know what they were.

Utterly beaten, he allowed me to pull them up his legs. Then I revealed the true purpose behind them: A waist chain and padlock. Ben now had absolutely zero access to his diaper area.

Then I left him to a chair and pulled him into my lap. I pulled a blanket over the both of us.

"There you go, baby. Cuddle close to Mommy. That's it. What a good sissy!" I stroked his cheek and kissed his forehead.

Then I lifted my shirt and his mouth dropped open in shock as I released my boob, and pressed the nipple into his mouth.

His eyes closed and his heartbeat slowed as I rocked and nursed him to sleep.

"Such a good boy. Mommy's so proud of you. Mommy's got you. You'll always be my good boy. Ssshhh"

I kissed my sleeping baby's forehead again and tenderly held him close as he nursed and napped for the first time. I used my free hand to snap a picture of the sleeping sissy, swaddled, sleeping, and gently suckling his Mommy's breast. THIS is what I'd really wanted when I started him on his journey.

I looked at the condom on the floor, still full of jizz. At lunchtime Ben would be getting a BIG surprise.

Ch 5: Finishing my Baby Workday

I opened my eyes to see Molly/Mommy looking down lovingly at me. I'd actually slept better than I'd had since Thursday night.

"Wakey wakey my darling." She said softly, running her fingers through my hair.

"I know you love to nurse on mommy, but Mommy isn't lactating yet, and baby has to eat!"

I whimpered as she pulled her soft, warm, comforting breast from my mouth with a pop. I wanted more. It felt so…right to suckle.

She picked me up and placed me on the floor like an infant.

"Sit here and be a good baby. Mommy will make you a little treat."

My stomach turned as she picked up the condom full of my cum, and poured almost all of it into the lab blender that we used to lyse cells. It was followed by a slice of cabbage and blended into a smooth paste.

She then dropped the entire condom into a glass of water and stirred it. The water went foggy as every bit of cum diffused into it. Then she threw the condom away.

"Now then. This is a little experiment. I'm betting you'll love your meal far more than this." She unwrapped a candy bar.

"Here comes the airplane!"

I opened and took a large bite of the candy bar. It tasted bland, and became a flavorless mush as I chewed. I forced myself to swallow it.

"Now…"

She lowered a heaping spoon of the mush to my mouth. I tentatively opened up and winced as the slop made contact with my tongue.

I'd expected musky, salty, disgusting slime tasting lightly of cabbage. And I was right, but somehow It also tasted like all the elements of Saturday's pizza and Sunday's omelet…but far more concentrated…I couldn't describe it. Did everything taste mildly of cum? Or was cum just that strongly flavored?

I'd expected to gag, cough, vomit, or SOMETHING along those lines. Instead it felt like I'd been microdosing dilute concentrations of semen all weekend.

Molly giggled, my confusion must have been painted on my face.

"Let me guess. You HATED cum the first time you tried it. Then everything else lost it's appeal and tasted dull in comparison?"

I didn't want to agree. But there was no way I could say yes without looking like a total cum dlut. I nodded slowly.

"I bet if I offered you a pepperoni pizza, or a pizza slathered in cum, you'd choose the latter."

Another scoop of the mush entered my mouth. It WAS the most flavorful thing I'd had in days. I hated that she was right. I was already so tired of tasting barely anything.

"It's nothing to be upset about, of course. It's the most natural thing in the world for a sissy. It's just a shame all that sissy cream you made over the weekend went to waste."

She offered me the final bite, and then the water which I guzzled down. I found myself sad that there wasn't more, and disgusted in myself for loving it so much.

Molly pushed the candy bar toward my mouth. I closed it tightly and turned away. More flavorless mush? Pass.

"That's my good sissy boy. Now let's try to get some work done." She patted my head and helped me to stand.

I felt my penis straining in it's plastic prison, but unable to feel the damp of my diaper. I could now move freely without simple movements stimulating me to the edge of orgasm. But by now I knew what I SHOULD be feeling, and that was enough to keep me constantly aroused.

The slippery satin and soft lace brushing andt my thighs also felt very taboo and oddly sexy. Until then I'd only associated the material with lingerie.

Throughout the day Mommy kept giving me hugs, playing with my hair or rubbing my back lovingly. Deep down I loved all this intimate attention.

Near the end of the day, Mommy asked if I'd brought spare clothes. I actually had, since I knew that my filthy diaper was bound to leak all over my sweat pants.

She looked disappointed when I pulled the jeans out of my bag, but delighted when they wouldn't fit over the diaper, no matter how hard I pulled.

"It's a good thing I brought you something, to be safe!" She presented a garment bag from the closet and opened it. My heart stopped.

Mommy walked beside me as we left the building. I attracted stares and giggles from everyone as I waddled along. She held my hand tightly.

I was wearing a white shirt with puffy sleeves and frilly lace around the cuffs. Instead of pants I had baby blue overall shorts with tiny white hearts printed all over them. The straps, pockets, and leg holes were lined with white lace. My shaved legs looked far more feminine and girly than I ever thought possible. I knew that I must have looked ridiculous.

From a distance you'd never be able to tell if my puffy diaper bulge hid a pussy or a penis.

The 'click-clack of my Mary Jane shoes echoed as we made our way through the building. I felt like I was on fire, I was so embarrassed.

Instead of the bus stop, Mommy led me to her expensive SUV.

"Come along, sissy. You're going to spend the night with Mommy."

My cock pushed painfully against it's confines. Sex with Holly? There was no way I could say no to that. I felt a little precum drip from my cage.

She opened the back door of her car and I climbed in, eager to be out of sight. As soon as I was seated she reached across my lap. At first I thought she was grabbing something next to me, but then-

Click

She'd just buckled me in! As if my ridiculous outfit didn't make me feel bad enough, a beautiful woman was treating me like a total infant! To make sure I was secure she pulled in the strap, tightening it around my waist.

sssssss

It was loud enough for us both to hear, as was the sound of my plastic diaper expanding against the rubber interior of the ruffled diaper cover. I shut my eyes tight in an effort to shut out the humiliation, and hid my face in my hands.

"Aww, is my little sissy embarrassed? Why? Doesn't the little cutie know that he was *made* to make widdle tinkles in his diapers?" She said, lifting my chin so I was looking up into her eyes.

"I-"

"Ssshh, it's okay sweetie. No talking for now. Mommy already knows. Maybe today's final gift will cheer you up."

I felt something being pressed between my lips, forcing my mouth open. At first I thought it was a finger, but as it pushed almost to my throat, and the plastic shield touched my lips, I realized what it was.

Despite my shock and the disgust I felt in the pit of my stomache, my stupid oral fixation had me sucking loudly on the phallus within moments of it entering my mouth.

"Now just sit there like a good boy and suck your binky. Mommy will take you home."

The drive was mostly uneventful, but I shrank into my seat, trying to futilely disappear at every stoplight.

The whole time my reflection stared at me in the rear view mirror. I just stared at the pathetic image of the sissy in the reflection, suckling on a rubber cock, hairless legs splayed open by a massive diaper bulge. Written in white on the oversized pacifier were the words "Mommy's Little Cocksucker."

Half an hour later, we pulled into the driveway of her large house.

This time I unbuckled well before she got to the back door. I had to do SOMETHING adult-like.

As she opened the door I hopped out, almost losing my balance due to the heavy diaper. I was eager to get inside and away from the eyes of the neighbors, however, Molly grabbed my ear with two fingers and held me fast.

"You unbuckled yourself! Bad sissy! What if we'd gotten into an accident!" She sounded genuinely surprised, angry, and worried for my safety.

Was she joking? Obviously I hadn't unbuckled while we were moving!

"Nod your head right now if you know what you did was wrong."

I hesitated, and slowly nodded. This wasn't enthusiastic enough for her.

"Do you?" She pinched my ear harder and pulled upward, forcing me onto my tip toes.

I squealed around the paci and nodded faster.

"Good boy. Let's get you inside."

I waddled behind her to the door. I prayed that nobody had seen me get scolded reprimanded in my lacey baby shortalls.

As we passed into her house I was temporarily taken aback by the expensive furnishings and decorations. Modern paintings probably worth more than everything I owned lined the walls in tasteful red and black.

She led me through her bedroom and into the master bathroom.

"Now, I'm going to take your diaper off, but first I want to make sure there's no poopies about to come out. Are you big enough to do some pushies for me?"

I nodded and scrunched my eyes closed as I strained. Nothing happened.

"I don't know what you're doing, but that's not pushing. I want to see my baby really try to make pushies. Squat."

I whimpered some kind of protest, but slowly lowered myself until my butt was nearly touching the floor.

"Now I want to *hear* your effort. Make noise so mommy knows you're trying."

I grunted and strained loudly in my new position, finally I felt the sensation of warm mush filling the back of my diaper.

"Good sissy. ***That's*** 'pushies'. If I EVER catch a diaper full of 'stinkies' or 'poopies' as you will refer to them from now on, and you haven't correctly done your 'pushies', you'll get a LONG and HARD spanking."

She grabbed the ring on my paci, and pulled the cock from my mouth with a 'pop'.

"Now tell me, *what did you just do?*"

I could have been tough. I could have just left the house. I think any other man would have at least put up some kind of resistance. But my butt was still stinging from the last spanking, my ego was in tatters, and I was so horny that I'd have said anything to get out of the locking diaper cover and cage.

"I-I d-d-did pushies. And I made s-stinkies in my diaper" I stammered out in a whisper.

"You did what now? I couldn't hear that."

"I did pushies and made stinkies."

"Say it louder. Much louder. With a smile."

I forced myself into making a grin. "I made pushies and stinkies in my diaper!"

"Perfect. Every time you fill your diaper, even if you couldn't control it, you will immediately do pushies to make sure you get it all out. And you will always announce your recent activities as you just did. Even in public"

I gulped. Every time? Even in public?

"Can I maybe- get a change? Please?" I asked as politely as I could.

She smiled. "You'll get a pass this time. In the future though, ANY kind of request or hint for a change will result in a punishment. Maybe a spanking…maybe just leaving you in your filth until you get a painful diaper rash."

I gulped.

"Nothing to be scared of. Mommy will take care of you. You need to trust in that. Now tell me, who controls when you get new diapers?"

"You do, Mommy."

She spontaneously booped my nose with a finger playfully, causing me to smile. "And don't you forget it, silly baby."

She helped me out of the shortalls and onto the floor. She removed a key from her necklace and used it to unlock the laced diaper cover.

She removed the diaper. I looked down to see the front, interior coated with precum, peel away from my body with a squelch.

Similarly to my last change she held my ankles over my head. I looked at my penis, swollen and stiff in it's cage, inches from my face. A drop of precum dropped onto my lips. I licked them. It wasn't as good as cum, but still better than any actual food I'd had in a while. Molly noticed what I'd done and smiled…proudly somehow, like an owner who's dog has done a trick on command.

Once I'd been cleaned I felt something cool and wet touch my hole.

"Pluggy time!" She said playfully.

I tried kicking and squirming away, but the only thing I accomplished was to wiggle my butt as her left hand continued to hold my ankles over my head.

"Ooh!" I exclaimed as I felt it press into me, forcing me to stretch open.

"Just relax, baby. Be a good sissy and take all of your little plug." She cooked softly

Little? It felt massive! I felt pain as she twisted it and pushed it in further and let out a whine.

Calm down. Just relax. You're doing so well, sweetie!"

Finally the largest part passed my sphincter, and my body sucked the remaining bit of the plug all the way inside.

A big spurt of precum dribbled from my cage. I made sure to catch it in my mouth.

"Now that your baby butt is nice and full you're ready for bath time!

A few minutes later I was sitting in a tub full of hot water with all kinds of floral-scented oils added to it. My paci had been pushed back between my lips, and I didn't dare to spit it out.

"Shower time for Mommy." She said.

She removed her shirt and bra, acting like I wasn't even there. My cage pulled mercilessly at my balls as she kicked off her pants and panties and did some stretches in front of me. When she bent over I saw everything…her ass, and her glistening, soft, moist, perfect pussy

I whimpered into the paci as my penis throbbed and struggled to reach it's full size. This was torture. Out of habit I reached down to touch myself, and only felt hard plastic.

She turned on the shower and I watched through the glass door as she rubbed soap all over her toned and curvy body. More than anything in the world I wanted to run my hands over her wet and soapy body, and bury my hard cock into her soft, warm pussy.

Several times she turned and smiled at me, obviously enjoying how sheepishly I sat in the tub, unable to do anything but impotently watch her.

After her shower she approached and began to bathe me slowly and sensually. Every moved oozed motherly dominance. She squeezed, from nded, and rubbed every inch of me. She giggled when I moaned, and kept me still by holding a fistful of my hair while she squeezed and rubbed my swollen balls and caged cock.If her goal was to make me feel like every tiny bit of me was her property it worked.

Once she was satisfied, she stood me up, dried me off, and led me to the bedroom. Before another pink diaper was taped onto me I felt her do something with the plug deep inside me before taping me up. She held up a silicone rod, The plug was now hollow! I realized that there was no longer any reason for her to remove it.

"In time we'll upgrade your plug until you forget what it feels like to ever not be stretched open."

What?! Was this pain really my new normal? There was no way I'd ever let this get that far! Sure I'd play along tonight, but by tomorrow afternoon I'd be back to my own apartment, cumming when I wanted, and changing my own diapers whenever I felt the need. My rebellious thoughts were interrupted.

"Would you like to join me in my bed, baby?" She asked, as she lay back seductively. My mouth went dry and a thousand horny thoughts flew through my mind.

I practically leapt into her bed. After a weekend of nonstop orgasms, a single day locked up was agony.

She removed my pacifier, and firmly guided me by my hair to her expost breast. I felt a jet of precum meet it's end in the pink padding taped between my legs. My cock throbbed painfully as I began to suckle at her breast.

"Good sissy. There you go. That's my baby."

I lay next to her, sucking at her right nipple. She pressed her right leg against my diaper, and I reflexively began to softly hump it. Damn this stupid cage! All I could feel was tight plastic as my frustration peaked.

Bzzzzzzzzz

While her right hand kept me pressed into her breast, her left hand activated a vibrator. If I pressed hard into her thigh, I could just barely feel the vibrations on my cage.

I whimpered pathetically as I realized she had no intent of ever letting me cum. This was the closest thing to sex she'd planned for me tonight.

After she'd moaned, bucked, anted, and sighed her way to multiple orgasms, she turned off the vibrator, but kept me latched to her nipple. I whined and continued my gentle humping.

"Aww, does Sissy want to make stickies in her Pampers? Are your little balls just sooo full of cream? Poor baby."

I nodded pathetically. I'd agree to anything if I could finally cum.

"Too bad you were a little bratty today. I think that only good sissy boys should get to make uncaged humpies. Don't you agree."

I tried to protest, but it came out as a mumbled whine that she interrupted.

"You see, sissy's exist to give pleasure and be obedient and useful. I think that the best way is to incentivize good behavior don't you agree?"

I was silent as I tried to interpret her meaning.

"A sissy gets nice sensual prostate milkings once a week. For health reasons. No orgasm, of course." She appeared to just be talking to herself.

"A caged or ruined orgasm should only get a sissygasm or ruined orgasm as a reward for overtly proving their sissyhood by serving and pleasuring others."

Was she reciting this from some book? Or had she been planning these rules for some time now?

"A full orgasm from stimming their little clitty is the **highest** honor." She looked down at me and played with my hair. "you'd have to fully impress me by being the sluttiest, most desperate little toy!"

I felt my heart sink. It sounded like I'd never cum again! Fuck this! Tomorrow morning I'd be out of here! I felt like my balls were going to explode *now*! There was no way I could wait a week just to sexlessly be milked!

"Ssshhh…calm your little head and go to sleep. Mommy's got you." She held me tightly and lovingly, and my rebellious thoughts were literally cuddled out of me.

I felt so cozy, so loved, and so warmly content to suckle at her breast. God, was I really a sissy baby? Was this really the life I was meant to have? Could I really be happy to live as Molly's submissive plaything?

I drifted off and slept under her loving gaze.

Ch 6: An Unplanned Retirement

As my sissy slept, suckling away at his Mommy, I used my phone to send an email from a fake company email. The first one would appear to be company wide:

To: All Staff (western branch)

As some of you may have seen, late Friday an employee was seen at work in clearly unacceptable and offensive attire. This attire was socially unacceptable, and did not allow this employee to conduct their laboratory duties in a sterile or capable manner.

Following an internal investigation and a meeting with management, the employee was identified and his employment terminated. We apologize for his blatant unprofessionalism.

-Your HR team.

This was followed by another to just him, outlining his termination and resources.

The next morning he was obviously distraught at having lost his job, but thankful that I allowed him to stay with me while I continued to go to work. Of course, he stayed locked in diapers and chastity.

Over the next week his amped-up libido had him begging and pleading so much for an unlock that I had to start punishing him for asking. If he wanted to cum he'd need to earn it.

None of his pants, save his sweats, would fit over his diaper, forcing him to roam the house in nothing but a t-shirt and diaper. I took this opportunity to fill his wardrobe with an array of embarrassing sissy clothing to accent his new life.He hated them at first, but with enough cooing and complementing, he slowly began to wear some of the less feminine options.

In my free time at work I'd put together a curriculum of sissy-school activities to train him, and I had new furniture coming every day.

By Friday, I'd replaced his bed with a crib, and professionally painted his room pink and white, complete with butterflies and hearts along the trim. He'd protested slightly, but caved when I suggested that maybe he didn't want his upcoming prostate milking.

Even though he didn't know it, the poor little baby would never be independent again.

Ch 7: Earning my Treat

I awoke in my crib. Bars over the top prevented me from leaving, They weren't locked, but I knew better than to leave it without permission. I usually didn't have to wait long.

The nursery light clicked on as Mommy entered the room.

"Wakey wakey! Is my sissy ready for her weekly reward?"

I squealed happily from my penis gag. Now that I thought about it, my paci rarely left my mouth outside of meals. If it was Mommy's plan that I become skilled at squeaks, grunts, moans, and squeals…it was working.

Mommy opened the top of the crib and lowered the railing. She guided me to the changing mat. I squated, unprompted, and made 'pushies'.

"Good baby!" Mommy said, rubbing my back while I made a concentrated effort to fill my already stuffed diaper.

"Ah mdth puhthees n thinkieth, Ommy!" It's strange, the more you say something with fake enthusiasm, to real excitement and congratulations, the more you mean it. A week ago I'd forced myself to announce my stinkies, but now I *actually* got some kind of weird excitement to make Mommy happy.

"What a good little baby I have! I'm so proud of you!" Mommy said happily, tossling my hair. "Now let's get all those poopies cleaned up and you can get your milkies."

Once my diaper had been removed and I'd been wiped clean, Mommy held my aching balls and rubbed them softly.

"Aww, they feel so full! Is sissy excited to drain this pressure a bit?"

"Mmm!" I moaned enthusiastically.

She pulled the penis paci from my mouth and began to softly massage my balls. A stream of precum began dripping from my clitty.

"I don't know…do you *really* need to be milked?"

"Oh yes Mommy! Please Mommy! I need my milkies so badly! Pleeaase!" I was groveling and simpering desperately like I knew she liked.

"Well I suppose you've been behaving alright…for your first week. But if I give you a milking you'd better promise to do better this week. That means NO spankings or punishments. And I'll be starting your training in earnest. Think you can be an extra submissive little baby for Mommy this week?"

"Yes Mommy! Anything! I'll be so good for you! Just please! My balls-"

Ahem

"Sorry Mommy, My little sissy grapes are so sore!" I pleaded.

She stuck the paci back into my mouth. I automatically sucked vervently on it.

"Present."

I flipped over and assumed the position of 'face down, ass up'.

Mommy giggled "your little plugged butt looks so cute stuck in the air! It's adorably framed by your frilly dress and petticoats!"

I winced as I heard the shutter sound of her phone camera.

I felt the tunnel plug within me pull outward

"Oh!" I exclaimed as it was slowly extracted, leaving my hole(most-likely) gaping. It had been days since I'd felt the relief if not being plugged. Shortly afterward I felt a thin plastic tool slip into me. I could only just barely feel it.

It pressed something inside me and my clitty pulsed in it's cage. It pressed that spot again, and my clitty throbbed

"Shhh, there's a good sissy. Just relax. Let Mommy know if you're gonna cum."

I felt pressure building in me, then it would suddenly release. I kept feeling like I was peeing or something.

I'd never been milked before. I had no i deal what to expect. I'd thought it'd be something extremely pleasureable, but this felt…odd and joyless. I felt like a barn animal being milked for maintenance reasons, not pleasure.

I moaned out my frustrations into the paci and began choked back tears. It wasn't fair!

"Mmmmmmph *sob*"

"Stay still, sissy. You're doing so well. We've only just started."

The slow throbbing, pressing, and stroking of my prostate continued for nearly an hour. If only she did it harder, or faster, or with a larger tool! Anything would be better than this slow carefully methodical procedure.

Finally, after my knees and elbows were sore from maintaining the position, the tool was removed.

"Time for a plug upgrade!" She said cheerfully.

Once again I strained and squealed as an even larger tunnel plug was slowly forced into me, stretching me wider than I'd ever thought possible. As my anus passed the widest part, it sank home, and I felt a squirt of precum as it pushed hard against my prostate.

"Stand."

I turned and stood, tears in my eyes.. From her kneeling position she removed a condom she'd rolled over my clitty cage.

My eyes went wide. The condom was half-filled with my own jizz! I'd never seen so much cum in one place in my life! Now that I thought of it, the dull ache in my abdomen and balls- er…sissy grapes was gone. Unfortunately I still felt just as horny as I'd ever been.

I began to cry.

"Now now, baby, it's okay! Shhh c'mere cutie."

I sat on her lap and she held me as I sobbed into her shoulder

"That was the bare minimum reward. Trust me, sweetie. If you're good, REALLY good, you can cum any way you like!"

"I wanna cuuummmm!" I sobbed, the pacifier falling from my mouth.

"I have no doubts that you're gonna cum so much once you're fully trained! Don't you worry about that my sweet. My baby. Shhh" she cooed.

"Mommy might know of something you can do tomorrow to earn the right to make stickies in your diaper…but if you agree there's no backing out." She pulled me away just enough to bring my chin up to meet her gaze.

"Please, Mommy! I'll do anything you want! Please!"

"That's my good boy." She pulled me into her shoulder and held me, patting my back motherly.

We stayed like that, her rocking me on the nursery floor until I calmed down. Then it was back into a fresh diaper and locking diaper cover.

Before I was left to my own devices, Mommy rolled the condom over the silicone dildo of my pacifier, and used a needle to poke a tiny hole in the tip of the condom.

I obediently opened my mouth as she pressed the foul object in. As I sucked a tiny droplet filled my mouth with a salty flavor. This time, due to how long I'd stayed chaste, it tasted ten times muskier than the last cummies I'd eaten. I coughed and almost spit out the object as a reflex, but barely managed to keep sucking.

"Good sissy. Don't you worry. After tomorrow you'll most-likely be a pro at eating semen.

I spent the rest of the day frantically wondering what she had in store for me,

The next day I was awoken early by Mommy, who pulled me out of my cozy crib at 5am to put makeup on me for the first time. I was still so sleepy. I don't know how long she spent working on my face.

Layer after layer was applied to my face with bristles, brushes, and sponges. She held me tightly by my hair as she applied mascara and eye-liner.

Then she put an outline, base, top, and gloss onto my lips, before spraying me with something to make it all set. When she felt done with that she turned me head left and right, brushing and plucking to make sure every detail was perfect.

"These will be for your reference, when you're learning to do this yourself." She said as she took some pictures of me from different angles.

Then she brushed my hair and added a babyish tiara. Finally she dressed me in a sissy version of a schoolgirl uniform.

It was pink and white, and covered with lace frills. "Mommy's Boy" had been embroidered across the shirt, and the micro skirt did nothing to hide my poofy diaper cover. If anything it just accentuated it.

A pair of knee-high socks and shiny mary-janes completed the horrifying look.

When I was shown a mirror I almost screamed. My mouth opened but nothing came out.

If it weren't for my flat chest NOBODY would suspect I'd been born male. My face had been painted to give the appearance of thick lucious lips, and my cheeks looked round and soft.

The overall impression was of a very cute young woman desperately trying to look like something from a porno. If I'd seen my current state in a bar a few weeks ago, I'd have pointed and laughed…but my cock would have started to swell.

My clitty throbbed in it's cage as I saw the sexy sissy in front of me.

"Mommy! I look-"

"Yes, cutie. Mommy knows. Now let's get you into the car. I still have to drop you off before I go to work."

"Drop me off? Where? Like this?!"

"Of course! How else would I drop you off? naked?"

I realized that from now on **this** was 'dtessed'.

"But-"

"No more talking. Only 'Yes Mommy' until I pick you up after work."

I nodded. "Yes Mommy."

I wet myself again as tightly buckled me into the back seat, and in 30 minutes we pulled in front of what appeared to be a large, skeevy sex shop in the more run-down section of town.

After she'd promised me the ability to make cummies I was determined to be obedient as she opened the door, unbuckled me, and led me by the hand into the building.

I blushed, as the cashier giggled upon seeing me. This was the most ridiculously feminine I'd ever looked, and I couldn't believe I was dressed this way in public.

Mommy led me to the bathroom, where she changed me right there on the floor, but before taping me into the new diaper she inserted a new toy I hadn't seen before.

She pretended not to notice my moan or twitching cage as she pushed it all the way into me.

In the back of the store was what appeared to be two phone booths next to each other, but the glass was painted opaque for privacy in one.

She opened the clear glass door of the right booth. There was a…*thing* hanging down from the transparent plexiglass wall dividing the two booths. It had straps on the end.

A collar with a chain lay on the floor. I had a bad feeling about this.

She pushed me gently to my knees, and locked the collar around my neck. The chain was bolted solidly to the concrete floor. Standing was no longer an option.

I looked at the tube-like thing in front of me. A droplet of something slimy dripped from the opening onto the floor in front of me. I suddenly realized what it was.

"Mommy! Please! Don't- Aaauuffff!"

The end of the fleshlight, which turned out to be combined with a ring gag on my end, was forced between my painted lips. My mouth became filled with the scent and taste of cold jizz and disinfectant. With a click, the Fleshlight straps were tightened and locked around my head

"Mmmmffhh mmmm-mmmm!" I wailed in protest as I clawed at the gag and collar futilely, I thrashed around but nothing budged.

"Are you done with your hissy fit?"

"Mhmm" I moaned pitifully.

"This is a cum training device. People that want to learn how to appreciate eating cummies actually willingly lock themselves here. Only I can undo the lock on your booth, though. I've arranged that. The store owns the key to the other side. They keep a list of clientele that are STD free. Anyone on that list may make use of that silicone pussy you're sucking on." She explained.

I hadn't even noticed I was nervously sucking!

"The fun part is that unlike a standard glory hole, the silicone vagina only reaches the tip of your tongue, and

your open mouth makes it hard to swallow. I'm afraid
you'll have no choice but to let cum ooze across your
tongue and fill your mouth all day. Besides, this is better
for you, since you'll need training before you're ready to
give a solo blowjob."

She held up a small remote.

"This is a remote to the vibrating dildo in you currently.
I'll leave it up to the real men to decide what pleasure
level you deserve."

She fed it through a slot in the dividing wall. I watched it
clatter to the floor on the other side.

"Bon appetit, sweetie!"

"Mmmmmmmph! MPH!"

My screams were ignored as Mommy closed the door
and locked it, sealing me to my fate of being
entertainment for the entire store.. I heard her call:

 "I'll be back at about five thirty! Have fun, sissy!" And
she was gone.

Despite my situation, my sheer horniness was in control.
The feeling of being trapped and forced to service men
had never been a fetish of mine, but I felt my clitty
pulsing and throbbing with excitement. This situation
was so strange, and so taboo. It didn't feel real.

I supposed that when you live a kinky lifestyle it's only a matter of time until you start to enjoy the kinks more as your inhibitions fade. I'd also found myself painfully hard when being humiliated, and I now accepted, and sometimes even enjoyed saying baby words to make Mommy happy

But this? Could I really enjoy this? I looked at the mirrored back of the booth opposite me. I looked equally sexy and adorable.

With some shame, I was forced to admit that if I had a little slut like that kneeling before me, I'd probably be nutting down her throat in seconds.

I could do this. I'd make Mommy so proud of me she'd HAVE to let me cum!

My self reflection was interrupted by a click as the booth opened, and a man entered. I blushed and felt white hot shame through every nerve in my body. My toes curled and my clitty pulsed.

Heavy tinting of the glass made it impossible to see him from the chest up, but I could feel him looking down at my helpless state and I heard him chuckle. For the first time in my life I knew what it felt like to be truly objectified. I wasn't even a plaything or a toy for this man, I was just a cute place for him to deposit a load of cum on his way to work.

I shuddered as I watched him unzip. He lowered his pants and underwear.

I stared at the thick cock and tried to pull away as it pushed slowly into the wall- mounted pussy. I whimpered as it snaked down through the silicone. The penis *almost* reached my mouth. I shuddered as I tasted my first drop of another man's precum.

 I watched as the pace increased. I shut my eyes , buct could still hear the thumps of his hips against the glass, and the squelch of his cock in the silicone sleeve.

Finally he thrusted hard against the plexiglass, and I felt the warm trickle of cum into my mouth. I screamed and thrashed against the steel collar. and pulled at the straps holding the Fleshlight into my mouth.

Despite my fit, my mouth slowly filled with warm, salty cum, but I could only swallow the part of it that reached the back of my throat.

I shuddered and coughed. It wasn't so much the taste. I'd already gotten used to the taste of cum since everything now tasted mildly like it. My disgust came from the simple fact that I was swallowing a stranger's cum.

I thought I heard giggling…laughing…talking? I was sure of it! I realized that there must be a few people watching the show, but I couldn't turn my head to look. From the voices I guessed there must be at least 5 people enjoying my disgust.

The man left, and was quickly replaced by another man, who was much shorter, younger, and extremely overweight. His cock only made it a few inches toward my mouth, and it wasn't long until I heard him moan, and watched a new wave of jizz spurt into my mouth to mix with the partial load. Still coating my mouth.

As I publicly and loudly filled my diaper, something broke inside me. My ego was non-existent, any pride I had left was gone. I didn't cry, what was there to cry about? In my mind I'd hit absolute rock-bottom, a week ago.

After the fifth load of slime entered my mouth I was finally coming to terms with what I was. I was incontinent. I was girly. I had a taste for cum. It had no job or career. I was taken care of by a dominant but kind mommy. And now, finally, it was sinking in that I only existed to give pleasure to men…real men. This was the only career path for someone like me.

It's amazing the attitude change that a bit of acceptance can give you. I'd been living as a man forced by circumstance to be a sissy. Now it was sinking in that I WAS a sissy. And judging from my reflection, an extremely attractive one.

I know it sounds sick, but I actually started to enjoy myself. Any real man reading this would never understand, hell, I think only another sissy would.

I looked at the reflection of the pathetic, sad sissy. I decided that I wasn't going to be **that** anymore. I modeled a smile. God, I looked so sexy I wanted to be one of the men using my mouth.

It had been a week since I'd seen any kind of porn. It sounds stupid writing it out now, but I felt my clitty throb as I watched the sexy sissy smile. I dissociated and began doing what looked hot. As another load entered my mouth, I began licking the inside of the fleshlight, and lowering my head to get every drop, moaning like a massive slut.

The next man noticed the small remote on the floor. He picked it up and turned it to high.

"Mmmgh!" I moaned and pushed my hands against my diaper as I writhed and humped against my hands. I cursed my stupid plastic clitty cage for what was probably the millionth time.

"Can you cum from this?" He asked.

I didn't think so. Probably not…it felt amazing though… maybe? I shrugged. I remembered that I was trying to be cute and sexy, and quickly followed it with a giggle.

"Well if you're good, maybe I'll leave it on this setting."

He unzipped and a massive cock sprang free from his boxers. I felt the Fleshlight expand as the phallus snaked down its length.

I was shocked when I felt the head of his penis pop into my mouth.

Remembering the vibrator setting depended on his happiness, I moaned happily and beamed as I licked the precum from his slit.

He ban to slowly thrust, and I did my best to maintain happily moan and rock back and forth, slurping on his cock to the best of my ability.

After some time, the cock pushed into my mouth and jet after jet of hot cream filled my mouth and ran down my throat. My cheeks bulged. I had to swallow multiple times. After I'd take all his cum, I licked and cleaned his tip before he withdrew his cock.

"Hmm. Not even a thank you?"

"Ank oo!" I said, smiling as widely as I could.

"Mhm."

He turned the vibrator to a medium setting and left. I was disappointed that my performance hadn't been good enough. Even though there was no way I could cum from this it felt good to rock back and forth on the vibrating tunnel plug though.

For the next few hours I sucked, licked, giggled, and begged for cum like I would have never imagined doing when I'd woken up that morning. As I practiced, the vibrator was left on high more often.

My diaper became so slick with precum. I kept humping the slippery padding against my hands. I kept Imagining how amazing it would feel, and how quickly I'd cum if only I could feel something besides a dull ache and hard unyielding plastic. When I wasn't humping both my hands I was using one or both to massage and stroke the cocks through the fleshlight to help them orgasm sooner. It became a game of seeing how quickly I could make a man lose control.

One man didn't even cum. He just pressed the tip of his flaccid member into the fleshlight. Just as I began to wonder if he would get hard, I heard a trickle, and a stream of urine began to flow into the rubber pussy.

In the split second before it reached my mouth I looked at the slut in the mirror. She'd been giggling and cum-drunk for hours. How should she react?

Surprising even myself, I giggled and swallowed the accrid taste. I beamed and rocked on my diaper. I could barely taste any urine, it was mostly just the trace salty and musky components. The smell was different though, I could smell the urine very strongly, but I felt pride in myself for maintaining my slutty disposition despite it. I even grinned stupidly

"Ank oo! Oh uh!" I don't know if anyone could really understand my 'thank you so much' but the sentiment always made it through.

This set off a trend for a short while of men finishing or starting their session by relieving their bladders into me.

Luckily it stopped before my stomach became too full. I had a feeling the store manager had put a stop to it.

I don't know how many more men I took, but by the time I heard the door unlock, my diaper was overflowing, the battery in the vibrator had died, and I had legitimately started to love watching my reflection, making the girl in the mirror do everything I'd dreamed of a girl doing to me.

I stretched my jaw open and closed, as Mommy pulled the fleshlight from my aching jaws.

"Mommy!" I squealed excitedly as I hugged her legs.

"Aww, did you miss me sweetie?"

"Yes, Mommy! I missed you so much!"

The fleshlight shook as another cock entered. I looked up at Mommy, then tore myself away from her.

"Look, Mommy!"

I willingly took the damp, drool-covered fleshlight into my mouth and began eagerly sucking. I didn't even stop when a steady flow of yellow fluid entered the tube. I gulped it down greedily, humping one hand while I moaned and stroked the cock through the clear silicone tube. I squeezed every drop of urine from the hardening penis.

Within 30 seconds, the cock pulsed, the man's crotch pushed against the glass of the booth, and I began to slurp and lick the inside of the fleshlight, eagerly licking out every bit of my reward.

Finally able to speak, I pulled my mouth away.

"Thank you so much for the yummy drink, and thank you especially for your delicious cum!" It felt good to finally be able to speak. I looked at the slut in the mirror. She was perfect. She was proud of her status. She'd accepted her role and loved being the best at it. That slut was me.

"Good sissy! Now let's get you home! You've earned a whole 10 second uncaged in your wet diaper!"

"Oh thank you Mommy! Thank you so much!" It was more than generous. I couldn't imagine lasting longer than 5 seconds in my current state.

"And since you love your yellow stinkies, you should have no problem eating your sissy cream from your diaper."

"Oh yes Mommy, thank you Mommy!"

Mommy reunited me with my paci and I happily sucked it as we walked to the store exit. Mommy was approached by the cashier, who offered her a wad of cash.

"That's one keen little slut you've got. Here are the 'donations' she earned from visitors."

"No need, keep it for yourself. Consider it a tip." Mommy said, gently pushing the money back to the girl.

"Wow! Thank you so much!"

"Haha, how did my sissy do? Did it take long to break?" Mommy asked conversationally

"Oh no! He might have been the fastest I've seen! I don't think it took more than half an hour before he was guzzling cum happily."

"Aww, you did so well!" Mommy said, tossling my hair.

"Once he's well trained you should schedule him for a saturday." The cashier said.

"Oh?"

"We remove the fleshlight on Saturdays. It's **very** popular."

Once we were home, and my diaper cover had been unlocked, mommy pulled my sopping wet, and slimy diaper cover from my body. I found the cold air uncomfortable.

My cock strained in the cage and I whimpered behind my paci as she turned the key in my chastity cage. Finally! I was going to cum!

"Ooh!"

Just the sensation of the tight cage slipping off my rapidly growing penis was enough to bring me to the edge. I'd been waiting for this for so long!

She pulled the diaper over my penis and taped it. Soft, wet, warm, squishy…it felt incredible to my attention-starved clitty.

She reached forward and lightly pressed on the front of the diaper with her pinky finger.

"Now then, are you ready to make stickies in your diaper for Mommy?"

"Yeth Mommy" I lisped, mouth still full of pseudo-penis."

"You have ten seconds…starting now."

I humped once, upward against her finger and was immediately brought straight to the edge of orgasm. No! I can't cum in two seconds! I need it to last longer! I slowly humped a second time, just enough to keep me on the edge.

Mommy giggled and pressed down hard with her single finger as my hips were moving upward.

"Noooo, Mommeee!"

The pressure was too much and I came. Hard. My mind went blank and I gasped for air. My hips thrusted back and forth into the air. I felt the results of my orgasm pulse out of me and flood my diaper.

I lay there motionless, barely aware of the diaper being removed, or the *click* of the lock as my cock, squished uncomfortably into the plastic tube, was locked back into it's home.

My soiled diaper was removed, my butt was wiped clean, and the diaper was placed next to my head.

"We'll, clean-up time!" Said Mommy.

I rolled over and looked at the white goo, coating the yellow padding. I refused to let myself look at the *other mess* on the other side of the diaper.

"We'll, hop to it, be a good sissy for Mommy!"

I slowly lowered my face to the diaper and began to lap up the slick coating.

"Aww, you're like a cute little puppy!" She clapped her hands excitedly.

Doing this degrading act while non-horny felt different and so much more real. This time I couldn't even retreat into horny fantasies.

I felt a tapping on my cage as it dangled between my legs.

"Aww, your clitty's all tuckered out and soft in it's tiny home. It's so much better like this! Don't you agree?"

"Mhm" I was barely listening.

She walked around and stood with one hand on either side of my head. I continued licking the diaper, my cheeks glowing with embarrassment.

"Missed a spot." She touched a small pool of cum with her toe. I moved there and quickly cleaned it.

"And my toe?" She lifted just her toes. Eager keep her happy and proud of me I quickly sucked her toe until I thought it was sufficiently clean.

"Good boy. Now why don't you give your diaper a big kiss and a thank you."

I leaned forward and gave the sloppy padding a small peck.

"Your diaper gives you a meal and holds your cummies and *that's* how you treat it? Show me how much you love it."

"I-"

"Are you gonna make an argument?" She said, in a tone of mock surprise.

I shut my mouth and then leaned down again, giving it a big sloppy kiss. I decided to use plenty of baby-talk words in my thank you to satiate Mommy.

"Thank you for holding my peepees and poopies, and thank you for being a plate for my yummy stickies."

"Aaaah! That was so cute! I simply **must** insist that you thank every one of your diapers from now on."

"Yes Mommy."

"Now over Mommy's lap for your spankies!"

"Spankies?! What did I do?!"

"Well, little one, let's walk through it. When I opened your diaper what did I find?" Her tone was that of a schoolteacher in a preschool.

My mind raced. "Poopies?"

"Yes! Well done, baby! What must you do before Mommy finds those poopies?"

"T-tell you about them…and the pushies" I whispered, looking at floor

"Very good! Mommy knew you hadn't forgotten! Now over Mama's lap!" She sat down on the nursery stool.

"But Mommy! I was-"

"You've just earned double spanks, sweetie. You may finish that thought if you think your little bottom can handle more."

"No Mommy." I resigned myself to my fate, and lay across her lap.

SMACK

The first spank with her open hand stung like crazy and made me suck in my breath.

"One. Thank you, Mommy."

SMACK SMACK SMACK SMACK

The spanking continued mercilessly at a smack per second on alternating cheeks. I had no chance to do the count and thank her.

SMACK SMACK SMACK SMACK

The stinging turned to a dull burning, stinging heat.

SMACK SMACK SMACK SMACK

The heat evolved into into an intense burn. I held out as long as I could. Surely she had to stop soon?!

SMACK SMACK SMACK SMACK

The spanking continued. Tears welled up and down down my cheeks and I kicked my legs futilely.

SMACK SMACK SMACK SMACK

"Aaaah!" I was crying now and didn't care how pathetic I looked. "Mommy please, I'm sorry!"

She didn't stop. I tried to crawl off her lap, but her left hand wrapped around my waist, and gripped my sissy grapes, using them to hold me tightly against her lap.

"Halfway there, sweetie."

SMACK SMACK SMACK SMACK

"AAAAH! I'm sooo- *sob* -ooorry!" I was bawling like…well…a baby.

The spanking still continues until I was squealing and sobbing incoherently.

Finally the spanking stopped and I was rotated to a sitting position on Mommy's lap. She put a finger under my chin and raised my gaze to meet hers

"Did my sissy-baby learn an important lesson?"

Y-yes *sob* Mommy."

"Good. I expect you'll **happily** take your spankings in the future, and **always** announce your bowel movements."

"*Sob* Yes Mommy."

"I'm not mad though. I couldn't ever be mad at my baby. I just want to raise you into a good sissy-baby."

She lifted her shirt and I found her nipple pressed against my lips. I began to suck greedily at it for the comfort that suckling gave me.

"There you go, cutie. I'm so **proud** of you! You did so well and drank so much cum today!"

"You were SO close to perfect. Mommy has to make sure you know when you do wrong, you know how much I want for you to be a good little sissy, right?"

She was so sincere…I actually felt bad for making her spank me. I temporarily stopped nursing.

"Yes Mommy, I'm sorry I was bad." I sniffed.

Once you've calmed down we'll get you ready for bed. Tomorrow your training begins. And I have no doubts that you'll make Mommy **so** proud!

Ch 8: Meeting Daddy

I was so proud of my sissy boy.

'Boy' was a stretch, though. At this point my baby didn't really conform to a gender. When he started his training a month ago he'd had the body of a boy, but now his clitty was the only remaining bit of male-ness about him.

He still believed he was a boy, but he now felt comfortable, and preferred his sexy sissy appearance.

A month had gone by, and I don't know if he ever really noticed how feminine he'd become.

His breasts had remained A cups. I'd lied and told my little sissy that cum naturally has estrogen in it and his favorite meal could be the cause. Faced with going cold turkey on his favorite flavor, he'd opted to keep the breasts, as long as they didn't get larger.

I suppose the transformation was just slow enough for him not to notice the softening and rounding of his facial features, or the redistribution of fat.

Even with no breasts at all you'd be hard-pressed to find a reason to assume he was male.

His gene therapy had changed how different parts of his body reacted to hormones, but his cock had remained the same unfortunately.

A week ago I'd snuck another treatment into his morning bottle of formula. His cock still got hard. His libido was still insanely high, but his cock had already seen the effects of the penile reduction treatment. I'd of course been keeping it a surprise. He hadn't seen his penis in at least a week. It's hard to get a view of anything through layers of petticoats.

In another month he'd be locked into a tiny flat cage. The only bulge in his diapers would be his set of swollen sissy grapes. The new cage sat in my dresser.

Some nights I'd just take it out and imagine his whimpers when I would eventually tell him his cock is now a stiff little nub, in need of a steel plate, not a tube.

I couldn't sleep. I opened my phone and began looking through various online shops at custom sex toys and bondage. Once I'd gotten bored and purchased more outfits for Sissy I began reading some intense and graphic mommy-domme erotica.

After a few stories I snuck to the nursery to check on my baby. He was fast asleep, his new larger paci pulsed in his mouth as he slept serenely. No doubt dreaming of cocks. After all, what else was there for a sweet little sissy-baby to dream of?

I returned to my bedroom and saw my phone screen light up.

I'd received a text on my phone. It was Jerry.

Hey, Just making sure that we're still on for brunch tomorrow.

I sent back:

Of course! I can't wait for Sissy to meet you!

Jerry was another researcher from another department at work. We'd met a couple weeks ago and discovered that we were both extremely kinky, and very into domming.

Now, after several lunches with him, I felt a strong connection and might actually be a little in love with him.

Feminizing and completely owning a sissy was a huge turn on, but no part of me wanted to have sex with such an unmanly little wuss.

No, my ideal relationship was with another dominant. I needed someone I could really connect with in every level. My sissy was just the perfect accessory to facilitate the lifestyle I wanted.

My ideal life was being a good wife, having fantastic sex, and taking out every drop of my dominant kinkyness on a third party alongside my husband. The beauty of having Sissy meant that I could effectively have a complete family dynamic without sacrificing any kinks.

I prepared a cup of tea and returned to bed. I fell asleep to fantasies of home-life with Baby and Jerry.

The next morning I prepped Sissy like I usually did for trips away from home.

After cleaning him, I used a white armbinder to secure his hands behind his back. Then I set one of his training devices in the middle of the room.

It was a princess-themed plastic potty, but I'd made a simple addition, a massive dildo riding straight up from the bottom of the potty. This device allowed sissy to sit and practice riding a cock for hours and hours, with any accidents being safely contained. Of course, he always had a soft silicone tunnel plug in as well to prevent his prostate from getting stimulated. 'Potty training' had a different meaning in my house.

"Sissy, Mommy has some good news for you."

He looked up at me and sucked on his penis paci nervously.

"You're gonna be a good little sissy and ride your practice potty. When Mommy comes back, she'll be bringing home a daddy for you to love!"

The paci dropped from his mouth.

"But- Mommy! What about us?!"

"Well, baby. Let's walk through it. Has mommy ever let you make stickies in her?"

"No, Mommy."

"How long did you last humping your messy diapers last time?"

"Not…not long."

"How long?" I asked sternly.

"Three-no-two seconds." His face flushed and he looked toward the floor.

"Is that enough time for you to even get inside of Mommy?"

"N-no"

I gave him a stern look.

"No, Mommy."

"So, even though I love you like my precious baby…what do you think a Mommy needs if she wants REAL sex, and not just nursies while she uses a vibrator?

"A daddy." He whispered it. This was probably verifying all his fears that while our relationship was close, kinky, and loving, it wasn't romantic, and barely sexual.

"Don't be sad, sweetie." I kissed the top of his head and hugged him.

I continued: "You've been practicing riding and sucking so much. I'm sure Daddy will love you and and be so proud of you!"

"But-but will you ever have sex with me when…when-he"

"Daddy" I said. "Daddy is both his name and pronoun to you."

"When you and he-" Sissy blushed. "Would you ever have sex with me?"

"Oh, honey." I said, dripping with pity. "Your stickies only belong in diapers with your poopies and tinkles."

I led him to the training potty and slowly pushed him down onto the dildo. He moaned as the tunnel plug stretched to accommodate the rubber cock.

I took his dainty, manicured hands and cuffed them to the sides of the potty.

"Trust me, baby. You're going to be so much happier with a real Daddy to help care for you."

"Yes Mommy." He painted as he sunk further into the dildo.

"I know you want Mommy to be happy too, right?"

"Of course, Mommy!"

"Well Mommy needs a real cock and a man to help her take care of you. Can you help make Daddy feel welcome when he comes?"

"Yes mommy. I'll try." He still sounded a little upset, but he understood and accepted it.

"Now Mommy has to go on a little date. I want you to bounce prettily for me and pretend it's Daddy. Be a good boy and do that for me."

Sissy cried out as I reached the nursery door. "Mommy! My paci!"

I turned and smiled. "Today you're gonna practice saying all kinds of pretty sissy things for Daddy. Think of what good slutty sissies should say. Say it all out loud for Daddy. Imagine his hard, powerful cock thrusting into you."

"Y-yes Mommy." He was so cute when he was flustered.

I paused before closing the door.

"And think hard and long on how a Daddy would want to be greeted by his new little sissy-baby." I said as I closed the nursery door.

***

We'd both greatly enjoyed the hidden camera footage of Sissy squealing and moaning in his girliest voice as he moved up and down. I loved how he'd held me tightly with his strong arms while I showed him the live feed on my phone.

"So even now he's plugged?"

"Oh yes. He's always got his tunnel plug in. It keeps him from ever stimulating his prostate enough to cum."

"That's so devious!" He laughed.

"I think of it like the plastic screen protector film on a new phone. His daddy should be the one to first make him cum from cock." I explained.

"Aw, that's so sweet." He said.

"How long will she- I mean he- practice while you're gone?"

"Until I get back..if he doesn't want a spanking."

Sissy had only once tried not to do training as instructed while I was absent. He'd earned a hard caning for that, which had left red stripes across his cheeks for a week. Now when I said to practice deep-throating while I was at work, he'd do it, even if I worked late.

"Why the restraints then?"

"His little clitty has been shrinking so quickly. I don't want him lifting his tutu and seeing it before you do."

Jerry laughed, a deep but kindly laugh. He'd make such a good Daddy for my baby, I thought

Jerry was nervous though. I didn't blame him. It was hard to be the new element in a relationship.

We met at my house and found ourselves creeping toward the nursery. We could hear Sissy crying out in ecstacy.

"Oh Daddy, please don't stop! ***moan*** "You feel so good, Daddy! ***Mmm*** "Fuck me harder, Daddy, Please!"

I opened the door.

Sissy froze.

I shuffled quickly into the room.

"Mommy's home!' I said as I quickly undid Sissy's hand restraints.

I returned to the entryway with an excited smile, and posed with my hands extended toward the door.

"Introducing your new Daddy!"

Daddy entered. His presence filled the room. At 6'5 he towered over Sissy and me. His manly beard and muscular stance was reminiscent of a lumberjack. Everything about him screamed 'macho' which only made Sissy and the rest of the room look more ridiculous and feminine in comparison.

"Daddy!" Sissy squealed happily. The dildo slipped from him with a pop. Sissy made a beeline to Daddy and wrapped his arms and legs around Jerry's. Sissy's face found it's way to Daddy's crotch where she began nuzzling and kissing his bulge through his pants.

"Hey there, baby." He said, rubbing Sissy's haid with one of his big callused hands.

"I'm so happy you're here, Daddy!" Sissy exclaimed. The baby was now breathing deeply of Daddy's cock through the material of his jeans, and it was clear that my little one's cum-lust was being piqued.

"Oh? Why is that? Daddy said."

"So you can make Mommy happy!"

"Do you not do that?" Daddy said in feigned surprise.

"I make her happy…in other ways."

Jerry bent down and picked up the baby, placing him firmly on his hip.

"What ways are those, sweetie?" He said, pinching Sissy's nose playfully.

Utterly taken aback at the extreme childish treatment from a stranger "Um- baby ways."

I could feel the connection forming. The submissive baby and dominant daddy. It was happening like I'd always dreamed.

"Uh, oh! Is that a wet spot I feel? I think someone needs a diaper!"

"I'll get him diapered." I said.

"No need, I can do it. I have a feeling I'll be doing this a lot." He chuckled.

Jerry walked across the room and placed our baby on the changing table as though Sissy weighed no more than a melon,

Sissy's clitty cage had been visible to us the whole time. Tutus do little to conceal anything. Despite this, daddy pretended to notice it for the first time.

"Well what's this, Baby?" He said, giving the cage a little wriggle.

"That's my clitty cage, Daddy."

"But why's it so big?"

B-big, Daddy?"

"Honey, would you be a dear and fetch the keys? Sissy needs an examination."

Very clever. By unlocking Sissyband showing we shared the key, he was showing that we were both sharing ownership.

"Of course, dear." I said, happy to oblige.While I was in the bedroom, I retrieved the tiny cage I'd been saving. The time was now.

I hadn't seen Sissy's careless cock since it was roughly the same size pre-trratment. I gasped and giggled as Daddy pulled the cage away.

Sissy gasped and painted, almost cumming just from the sensation of the tube being removed.

Daddy snaked the tutu down Sissy's legs, carefully not letting it touch Sissy's throbbing member.

"This is your cage" Daddy held up the three inch long plastic tube.

"And now look at your hard clitty."

Sissy lifted his head, and saw nothing. Panicking, he sat up and looked at his pathetic little penis.

It had shrunken, but the skin hadn't, giving the effect of a single inch of wrinkly flaccid-appearing cock.

"But but- but it-"

"Needs a new cage! That's right, sweetie!"

Daddy slipped the new ring around his large, sollen balls, and easily over his teeny micropenis.

"Say 'go home Miss Clitty!'"

"Go home, clitty" Sissy whispered, still in shock over how useless penis had suddenly become.

Sissy lay back and whimpered as the flat cage was pressed hard against his tiny stiffy.

"Mmm!" A final push forced the tip and ring to meet.

Daddy turned his key and taped up Sissy's diaper.

"Hmm, it looks like it came with two keys! Perfect for Mommy and I to split!"

Sissy squirmed and whimpered, trying to get used to the tight compression of his penis. A tear fell as he came to terms with the fact that the only thing his penis could ever be inside of was a cage or a diaper.

"Now now, don't fret. Daddy's got you."

He picked up sissy and soon had him sitting on his lap, looking into his eyes as he spoke.

"Your mommy claims that sometimes she tells you to do things and you hesitate for a few seconds."

A lie, but I knew exactly where he was going with this. He and I were in sync.

"She said that when I met you you'd need a break caning as hard as I could."

"Yes, Daddy."

Jerry held the baby, stopping him from rolling into his stomach for the spanking.

"I don't think that's entirely necessary. Instead, how about a mild hand spanking every day, just so you remember to do what you're told immediately. Would that be better, cutie?"

Brilliant. He was befriending my baby, establishing a routine, and building trust all at once.

"Y-yes, Daddy."

"Good boy….actually. I wanted to ask you about that."

"Daddy?"

"You live here in a pink nursery wearing dresses and diapers, knowing your little clitty will never ever see a vagina, sucking and fucking an endless stream of dildos, and if you're good you get to suck down anonymous men's cum as a treat. Is that all correct?"

"Yes, Daddy."

"But if you're a straight man, why didn't you leave before it reached this point?"

"I-I have no job! I'm incontinent! I'd be lonely and homeless!" Sissy exclaimed.

"Now honey," Daddy began to explain, in the tone a patient father uses with an unreasonable child. "There's not a single man I know, myself included, who'd prefer to live in your current conditions over being homeless."

"But I-I…I.." Sissy faltered. He hadn't expected an interrogation today.

"Face it. You might not have been kinky before, but when Mommy put you over her lap and spanked you for the first time, your little clitty got all excited and drippy, didn't it?"

"I-I"

"No need to explain. Daddy knows."

He raised Sissy's chin, and he looked kindly and sympathetically into Sissy's eyes

"Daddy knows. You're not the first little sissy I've seen discover themselves. But you are the cutest." He tickled our baby's tummy, making him giggle and laugh.

"Daddy stop!" He said, squirming and giggling on Jerry's lap.

Jerry stopped and looked serious again.

"Your name is Ben, but I get the feeling it no longer makes you comfortable. Does it make you upset when you are forced to think of yourself as a man? When all you have is a drippy clitty?"

"How did- I mean…yes, Daddy."

Jerry stood, and placed Sissy on a stool in front of the floor-length mirror, and pushed the penis paci into his mouth.

"Now Mommy and I are going to go watch a movie. I want you to look at yourself in your princess dresses and think of a name suitable for such an adorable little sissy-baby, one that makes you comfortable, one that makes you feel like the sweet cum-slut you want to be."

I met Jerry by the nursery door, we turned and looked at our little baby, who was staring intently at the feminine slut in the mirror. It was quite a sight. Pigtails on either side of his head, face painted immaculately, and a pink shirt and tutu above a massive princess-themed diaper that spread his legs wide. Knee-high socks and shiny mary-janes completed the look.

I broke Sissy's concentration.

"Please don't feel like you need to make any decisions tonight. We just think that you might need some time to think some things through. We just want you to be comfortable."

And with that we were out of the nursery.

"So..Movie?" Said Jerry.

"Later. Seeing you in daddy mode has me all hot and bothered. You're coming to the bedroom first for a good fucking."

"As you wish, he chuckled as I led him to my room.

The sex was incredible. It felt amazing to have a partner as dominant as myself. The session with our sissy had made me so wet, and him hard as a rock. He pumped deeply and quickly into me, both our minds filled with nothing but pleasure. It had been so long since I'd had a real man as masculine and powerful as him.

It was a little more than two hours later when a very shy and embarrassed looking princess/baby/ballerina shuffled into the living room. Jimmy and I were halfway through a movie.

Jerry and I looked up at the little sissy, who was a little shocked to find Mommy and Daddy completely naked. I patted a spot on the floor in front of us. Soon the vacant spot at our feet was filled with a freshly damp diaper.

"Pansy." Murmured the newly self-christened Pansy.

"Sissy-baby Pansy! What a beautiful name! And it suits you so well!" I said.

"Yes, it's a wonderful name! We're both so proud of you for taking such a big step!"

Pansy looked up at us and bit her lip. I thought I detected a tiny shy smile.

"Any thoughts of your pronoun preferences?" I asked.

Pansy blushed. "I thought for a while that I was a boy, and I still do sometimes…but I think…I think-"

"Yes sweetie?"

"I think I'm a daddy's girl." She blurted out, quickly getting the words out. She blushed hotly, and planted a quick peck on the tip of Jerry's penis.

"Aww, that's so cute!" I exclaimed.

"Well then, I guess I now have a babygirl! It's a shame we just finished having sex. I don't know if I-" Said Jerry.

"Please? Maybe I can make you cum again?"

"Sorry, baby. Daddy's cock belongs to me tonight. You may help yourself to the used condoms in the bedroom garbage though. And afterward you can suck on Daddy's balls to help him relax."

"Yes, Mommy! Thank you Mommy!"

We watched our Sissy scamper out of the room to drink the condom contents.

"Well I think that went **VERY** well" I said.

We spent the rest of the day cuddling on the couch. Our sweet baby Pansy fell asleep with her mouth full of Daddy's balls, his semi-hard cock resting on her forehead. Her face was become painted with a film of precum.

I *had* to take a picture. It was too cute.

***

I was sucking a sloppy wet cock that kept spurting over and over again. It kept shooting jet after jet of delicious cream Into my mouth faster than I could swallow. Drool and cum dropped from my face and onto my chest. I realized that it was covering the floor and filling the room. I needed to leave but couldn't stop sucking, it tasted so good and felt so good to slurp on.

I awoke face down on a pillow soaked with my drool. My penis paci had fallen out in the night.

The haze of sleep slowly slipped out of my mind. I felt a warm mess in my diaper. Automatically I got onto all fours and did some pushies. My diaper expanded outward behind me, before the mess fell downward, causing my diaper to droop low within my pastel onesie.

Mommy entered the nursery followed by Daddy.

"Mommy! I did pushies and made stinkies!" I happily announced. I'd never get used to doing that, but I think that was the point.

"Good girl." Daddy said.

"Someone slept so deeply nursing on Daddy's balls! He had to carry you to your crib" Mommy said as she lowered the railing.

Daddy picked me up and put me on the changing table where Mommy began prepping my morning change. They were like a perfectly oiled machine. The perfect duo, happily taking care of their submissive baby.

I looked down as cold air hit my sissy-grapes. I could no longer see a penis. My cage was so small that I could only see the steel plate covering my straining little clitty if I lifted my head, enough to look over my tiny baby boobies.

As the wet wipe rubbed my balls I whined piteously. God, I wanted to cum so badly. My sissy-grapes were heavy, swollen, and I was ever-aware of the pent up pressure, eager for any level of stimulation to let me cum.

I'd learned not to ask to cum. Good sissies wait patiently for their reward. Asking always resulted in spanking and a longer time between orgasms. If I was lucky I could gain the opportunity to hump my diaper once every couple weeks.

Daddy watched as I was wiped clean and taped into a new diaper. I rolled off the table and stood uncertainly in my new crinkly padding.

"Come here, sweetie. Daddy has a little treat for you"

I turned and saw Daddy, slowly stroking his long, thick cock.

My mouth began to water, and i dropped to my knees. It's amazing how much you crave the only thing you can really taste.

I approached and could smell the delectable precum. This was going to be the first REAL cock i'd be sucking.

My mind filled with hundreds of hours of sissy porn that i'd had to watch in preparation for this moment. As my lips approached the glistening head, I couldn't decide on how I was going to suck it. I felt anxious, butterflies filled my stomach and I thought I'd be sick. Here I was, a perfectly straight, previously normal person, willingly changing my name to Pansy and excitedly about to suck the cock of a man I only knew as Daddy.

I felt a spurt of precum in my diaper as my lips made contact with his soft, pink tip. I extended my tongue and looked up into his tender eyes as I gave his cock the sloppiest, wettest kiss I could.

"There you go. That's my good girl." His hand on the back of my head pushed me gently but firmly forward onto his shaft. My mouth filled, and I felt the tip press gently against the back of my throat.

"That's it. Open for Daddy." I inhaled, and with a gentle push, he entered my throat. I bobbed forward and backward on him. Every time I looked up I saw a tender gaze full of admiration and loving pride in me. All i wanted in that moment was to make him happy and be the 'good girl' he saw me as. I occasionally pulled off of his cock, to lick and suck his balls, but doing that time I always kept a hand stroking his slippery penis.

After a few minutes, I felt his balls tense. The first spurt coated the inside of my mouth. I moaned in delight as I savored every little component of the jizz.

"There you go, baby. There you go. Drink all your milkies."

"Mmmm!" I moaned happily, as I felt the thick cream roll around my mouth, getting ever fuller with each spurt.

I hated to do it, but I eventually had to swallow.

"Good girl. I'm so proud of you!"

Daddy stroked my head as I licked and sucked his head, desperate to get every drop I could from him.

"Now then. Are you going to be a good girl for Mommy and I while we're at work?"

"Oh, yes Daddy!"

"Aren't you forgetting something we talked about yesterday?" Mommy asked expectantly.

My mind raced as I thought out every single thing we'd done. I walked myself through the events of yesterday as fast as I could. I remembered and my stomach filled with trepidation.

"Daddy, May I have my daily spanking now please? To keep me good?" I spoke the words barely louder than a whisper. Asking for my spanking. I couldn't believe that this was my new life. I'd accepted it, and i suppose deep down I loved it, but still…the humiliation burned bright within me.

"Of course, sweetie. Over Daddy's lap. You've been such a good girl I'll go easy on you just this morning, but if you are naughty, it'll be harder, or with the paddle."

"Yes, Daddy. I understand."

I crawled across his lap, and felt cold air on my cheeks as the back of the diaper was pulled away from my exposed behind. As usual I remembered to keep count and thank him with each impact.

SMACK!

Daddy was so strong! It was only his hand, but it felt like a paddle! I winced and fought back the tears from the first spank alone.

"Mmmph! One! Thank you daddy for helping me remember to be good!"

SMACK!

"Ah! Two! Thank you, Daddy!"

The spanking continued until my bottom was bright red and stinking like it was on fire. It's a good thing that the diaper front was between me and Daddy's leg, or I know i'd have soaked his pants with the precum dribbling from my cage.

"Thank you so much, Daddy! I cried through tears as mommy taped my diaper up.

"I want you to practice deep throating and makeup today. And when I get back I'll be giving you a VERY personal examination to see how your riding lessons have been coming along

"Yes Daddy, thank you, Daddy!"

"See baby? I told you that you'd love having a daddy."
Mommy said as she wiped my drool from my chin. "Be
good now, byebye!"

"Bye Mommy, Bye Daddy! I love you!" I called out as
they left me alone in the nursery.

Ch 9: Justice For Pansy

Life with Jerry and Pansy continued in total bliss. He was a wonderful addition to the family, and he cared for Pansy as much as he did for me. All three of us were happier than we'd been at any point in our lives.

After a few months Pansy had begged to help around the house while we were gone, and Jerry had provided her with her very own maid outfits. They all were the very model of sissy fashion, made of various colors, but dripping with lace, bows, and not providing even a little bit of coverage for her thick, (usually full) diapers.

Every day we'd come home to a clean house, and Pansy on her knees by the door, eager to suck Daddy off in exchange for 'changies'.

Today though, something seemed off. Jerry had gotten home well before me, unusual since he'd always been working later than I due to his recent promotion.

I thought I heard some talking as I put my key into the lock, but it stopped abruptly as I opened the door.

"Honey! Baby! I'm home!" I called.

"In the dining room, dear!" Daddy called from the dining room.

I entered, and saw Pansy buckled tightly into her highchair sucking her paci; Daddy sat next to her. On the table between them was a small manila folder.

"What's all this? Bringing work home with you?" I asked as I pulled out a chair and sat opposite them.

"Well…You could say that I brought home with me to work, then some work back home." He said.

Something was off. Jerry was always super upbeat and happy to see me, but now he sounded…sad? Or was it hesitant. Either way there was something going on.

"Well, come on, you can tell me anything. Is something wrong?"

"I'd say a few things are wrong."

"Well? Honey?"

"As you know I was just promoted a couple weeks ago. Part of the procedure when there's a new head of genetic research is a total inventory of laboratory stocks."

"Oh. And?" I was trying to remain calm, and cool. Maybe he didn't know everything. Maybe he only suspected.

"There were the usual discrepancies that nobody cares about. But-"

"Something expensive missing?"

"No, nothing like that. And I think you might know where i'm going with this. The more i looked into the discrepancies, the more the dots started to connect. In short, I found out that you'd dosed your lab assistant."

"I-It was a spur of the moment thing! Pansy was just so cute and submissive! I know that's not a good enough defense, and i'm sorry."

His eyebrows raised. Pansy looked upset but not angry.

"We know you repeatedly dosed your assistant to create Pansy.

I was well and truly caught.

"The first time was a spur of the moment, but Pansy was so sad and distraught over the incontinence that I may have…gone overboard..a few times." My statement ended in a guilty mumble as I looked at the floor.

"Pansy and I have been talking. Most of these treatments are reversible, but only after millions of dollars in additional research."

"I-I know."

"And since Pansy and I still love you, and we don't want to see you go to prison, you've violated our trust, broken the law, operated well beyond the bounds of ethics, and twisted, if not broke, every rule of consent."

"Yes- I'm sorry." Tears streamed down my face and dripped from my nose as I looked at the floor.

Jerry continued.

"We still love you, but we can't trust you anymore. We don't want you to go to prison, but we also don't feel comfortable with you as Mommy, since you don't seem to respect others' consent. But..we both agree that you should be punished."

"I- I understand….how do would you proceed? If there's anything I can do to earn your respect and trust again, please…i'll do anything!" I looked up, tears were streaming from my eyes. My world was collapsing and I had nobody to blame but myself for my misfortune.

"We still love you. We still want to love you. But things will be different."

"Anything!"

"You have two options. The first is that you get justice from the law. You will probably face a sentence of at least ten years with good behavior. I would take Pansy and continue to care for her until your release."

"And the other option?"

"You reduce yourself to a person who couldn't hurt a fly. Someone we can both trust."

He placed a syringe on the table.

"What-what is that?" I asked, my voice breaking with adrenaline, fear, and despair.

"This..is full of that same incontinence treatment that you injected Pansy with so long ago. It also has a libido enhancer, a dilapidator, the nursing gene, the custom flavor edits that you pioneered, as well as a very experimental treatment for people suffering from Persistent Genital Awareness Syndrome."

"What? Persistent-"

"In summary, ilt will reduce sensation of your clit to nearly nothing, and heighten the sensitivity of your vaginal wall. You may be able to cum with a large enough object penetrating you, but that will obviously only happen when you've been good. It will be quite impossible for you to get any penetration through a locking diaper cover, and rubbing your diaper will never be enough to cum."

"But- I- that's- you'll effectively be turning me into-"

"Yes, that's right. You would be Pansy's little sister, and my second baby girl. The syringe will make you equally incontinent, and you will be naturally desperate to have sex with any kind of object or person you can get your hands on. It was the only option since your anatomy doesn't really allow for a clitty cage.

"You can't do this!"

"Oh, I can't? But you were allowed to?"

"I mean- it isn't that simple!"

"Isn't it?"

I saw that there was no use arguing. I'd been caught, and none of my options were good.

I sighed.

"How long do I have to decide?"

Jerry looked at his watch.

"Let's say…5 minutes. If you leave that door, you choose the government's justice. If you bend over the table, wiggle your baby butt and ask me nicely, I'll of course give you your medicine, and you can sleep with Pansy in the crib."

I bit my lip. I'd always had a tiny bit of a submissive switch side. Wouldn't a warm cozy nursery with my new family be preferable to prison? Maybe i would even like it.

I stood, lowered my pants and bent over. I moved my butt slightly and sobbed out a barely audible request.

"I'm sorry." Said Jerry. "I couldn't make that out."

"Daddy! Please give me my medicine!" I sobbed. Tears ran down my face. I had to admit as much as I hated it, this justice was perfect. Here I was begging for the exact treatment I'd non-consensually given to my laboratory assistant.

I heard him approach from behind, and felt the sting of the needle as it penetrated my right cheek. I could almost feel my adulthood slipping away from me as he pushed the plunger, filling me with the 'medicine' that would eventually make me a perpetually horny diaper slut.

"I'm sorry." I sobbed.

"I know you are sweetie." He pulled me into a hug. "Pansy and I are so proud of you for taking responsibility for your actions. You wouldn't have chosen the syringe if you didn't really love us and want to stay with us."

Pansy was smiling sympathetically at me, Daddy and my new sister both looked like they were about to cry from a mix of sadness at losing a Mommy and girlfriend, and happiness that we would still stay together.

Daddy returned to the table and picked up a second, smaller syringe.

"Wha- what's that?" I asked, fearing another surprise edit to my DNA.

"This one is for Daddy."

He turned it toward his thigh, stuck it into his leg, and pushed the plunger.

"Daddy!" Pansy and I cried out at the same time, and for the first of many times, I felt like the two of us really were his children.

"Now now, sweeties. That's just some of that same libido enhancer. After all, I have to keep both my babygirls satisfied, now don't I?"

I sadly realized that I'd lost my boyfriend, but I couldn't ask for a better daddy. What kind of wonderful person subjects themselves to experimental gene therapy just to make sure his babies get enough of their favorite flavor?

I glanced at Pansy, who was also staring at Daddy in awe of his decision.

Then I shuddered at the realization that I'd shortly be losing all taste except for cum, and then it would only be a matter of time until I craved to have a cock spurting into my mouth.

"Well then, come along my little ones!" He wiped away a tear. And unbuckled Pansy's highchair straps.

"Let's get you both changed and ready for bed!"

END

About the Author

I am write these stories while strictly locked in chastity. I apologize for any typos you may have encountered. I can't tell you how hard it is to concentrate on writing when my diapers/panties are soaked from my precum and my cage is pulling hard on my balls. (I'd like to see how well other authors can write under these conditions!)

For me, the sissy fetish was a stepping stone to realizing my true self, and becoming a happier, and more feminine person. I hope that this story helps others as they discover where their identities start and kinks end.

Thank you so much for reading, and I really hope you enjoyed it!

www.ingramcontent.com/pod-product-compliance
Lightning Source LLC
Chambersburg PA
CBHW061318120726
48001CB00002B/582